About the Author

Jaidz Majasi is a London-based children's writer. She is an accomplished primary school teacher and special needs coordinator, who has honed her craft over the last ten years whilst championing the benefits and beauty of storytelling with her students. When she is not writing or teaching, Jaidz enjoys reading, meditating and travelling to far-off lands to uncover the diverse and magical gems the world has to offer. Jaidz is a mother and an active advocate for positive mental health. She is also a qualified meditation instructor and practitioner.

To Jayda,

Jaidz. M

Mirror Maze Land

Jaidz Majasi

Mirror Maze Land

Olympia Publishers
London

A CIP catalogue record for this title is
available from the British Library.

ISBN: 978-1-83934-076-5

Bumblebee Books is an imprint of
Olympia Publishers.

First Published in 2021

Bumblebee Books
Tallis House
2 Tallis Street
London
EC4Y 0AB

Printed in Great Britain

www.olympiapublishers.com

Dedication

For Solomon and Sheila Majasi, a.k.a, Mama and Baba – my very first fans who inspired me to follow my heart and reach for the stars!

The New Kid

Zed was drenched with sweat and locked in a void of spiralling anxiety. The more he tried to conceal his inner turmoil, the more he perspired, causing a heatwave of embarrassment which was plastered across his face for everyone to see. He agonized over the impending moment that unfortunately for him, was inevitable.

Everyone was always curious about the new boy in school and for Zed, he had been that kid for most of his life.

Miss Kind, his newest teacher, said the obligatory, "We are lucky to have a new pupil joining our class today."

Her face beamed with pride; she could not contain her excitement, as she clasped her manicured hands together, clapping and squealing with delight.

No one could be that happy. Could they?

Miss Kind nodded at him in anticipation, as though she was waiting for her favourite movie to begin, and Zed assumed that it was his cue to introduce himself.

With the sole aim of making the experience as painless as possible, he knew he had to do it quickly, leaving no room for questions. He needed to sound dull.

Zed wiped his sweaty palms across his chest, took a deep breath in and on the exhale, he muttered, "You can do this."

Rolling his eyes up, he focused on a tiny crack in the classroom ceiling to lessen the effect of the glares of scrutiny which caused his skin to prickle.

"Hi," he began with a cracked and harsh tone, "I'm Zed. I have just moved here with my parents. I guess you could say I am good at drawing... um... yes... that's just about everything you need to know about me."

Relieved that the worst part was over, Zed retreated to his seat and focused on the ground beneath him. There was nothing fascinating about the blue and white linoleum chequered floor, but it was much more inviting than the stares of strangers.

Zed came across as rude and uninterested, which stunned Miss Kind. With little else to contribute to his abrasive presentation, Miss Kind smiled – unconvincingly – to ease the tension in the room.

"Well, thank you for that... um... interesting introduction Zed. I know that it can be an overwhelming experience having to start over in a new place and I gather you have done it quite a few times." She directed a sympathetic head tilt and faux-frown at him as she continued, "And to top it all off you are in Year six. That can't be easy."

Zed returned an unconvincing smile, hoping she would move on from him and teach them something – anything – as long as he didn't have to talk about himself, or read out loud. If there was one thing that Zed despised more than talking about his miserable existence, it was reading to an audience who were probably more competent readers. Nobody wants to sound stupid in front of their classmates.

Fortunately for Zed, Miss Kind turned her attention to another child. Quinton was a bold and popular member of the class; he embodied the term 'natural born leader'. Quinton spoke with a smooth buttery tone to his voice, and he seemed as excited about the world as Miss Kind, but in a laid back sort of way.

"Q?" Miss Kind hailed him. (Everyone called him that

because he was everybody's best friend.) "Would you be so gracious as to show Zed around today?"

"Miss Kind, it would be my absolute pleasure."

Q held his palms against his chest, exaggerated a bow and flashed his perfectly aligned white teeth.

Zed felt out of place.

He wished he could crawl into a tight dark space so he could just ignore the world and not have to reveal anything to those perfect individuals who appeared to be ridiculously enthusiastic about everything.

At break time, Q was eager to show Zed around. Although Zed was nauseated by the cheery characters, he agreed to take part in a "grand tour" led by Q and the five other hangers-on who followed Q wherever he went.

"We have to start with Mrs Long-Bottom's room!" Q insisted eagerly.

The headteacher's office? I mean who, in any realm or universe, gets excited about visiting the headteacher's office?

In Zed's experience, he had always thought of it as the place you visit before being sent home. What he hadn't shared with his class earlier was that he had studied the interior walls of more than a few headteachers' rooms.

Mrs Long-Bottom extended a bony limb towards Zed as she warmly invited him into her office. "I see you're getting the 'grand tour' from Q? We are all so pleased to welcome you into the Nerrison Primary School family." She peered down at Zed over her tiny spectacles that perched unsteadily at the very tip of her very pointy nose. "I have an open-door policy here at Nerrison and I do so hope that you can come to me with any questions or worries you may have."

Zed struggled to process that notion. He believed that she

was just putting on a show for him and as soon as he made a mistake or got overwhelmed – which he often did – he would be cast out of the 'Nerrison family'.

After his interesting introduction to Mrs Long-Bottom, Zed was further convinced that Nerrison wasn't the place for him.

Out in the playground, Q directed Zed's attention to a large boy who was parked on a picnic bench, devouring an apple, whilst rooting around in his ear for stray chunks of wax.

"Look at that one over there? That's Franky Hillson. Nickname's 'Hill'. I bet you can guess why?"

Zed rolled his eyes. *How original*, he thought to himself, but he managed to contain the expression, fearing he would alienate himself from his peers so early on in the school year.

"Um, I'm guessing it's because he is on the large side?"

Q and his companions erupted with laughter, and there it was. Proof that they were not as friendly as they all initially presented themselves as being.

It appeared that Hill did not fit in with them either and that intrigued Zed.

"So? What about him?" Zed probed for further information.

One of Q's friends, Trevor (clearly second in the chain of command), said, "That dude is one to stay away from. Whatever he wants, he takes. People find it hard to say no to him because they're afraid he'll hurt them, so we all stay away from him. He's in the other Year six class, so that's easy enough for us to do."

"So… has he ever hurt anyone?" Zed asked.

The boys stopped and pondered for a moment before they all arrived at the same conclusion.

"No!"

They muttered between themselves looking perplexed. The group refocused their attention on Hill who, still alone, appeared to be inspecting his arm, as though he were counting the freckles on his trunk-like limb.

Q felt the need to defend his character portrayal of Hill as he explained. "The reason Hill hasn't hurt anyone is because everyone leaves him alone. If he asks for something, we don't argue, we just give it to him. That is the way it has always been since nursery."

At that moment, Hill looked up and flashed Zed a half-smile before continuing to explore his skin.

Zed remained unconvinced by Q's case and the group's pack mentality. He had met a lot of bullies that pretended to be a teacher's pet, so he could spot them pretty soon after meeting them. Zed believed that Q and his friends needed to vilify someone to feel superior and it was unfortunate for Hill that he was their nominated villain. Hill was seen as an outsider and that is exactly how Zed felt.

The bell rang to signal the end of playtime, and without delay, all the children sauntered back to their classes.

"Well, I believe you all had a pleasant break time," Miss Kind began. "Now for some real fun! As you are all aware, this is your last year here at Nerrison Primary and all the other pupils, teachers and parents are expecting us to put on a spectacular end-of-year production. We will work with Yellow class when we rehearse, but first, we need to allocate the role of narrator. Isn't that thrilling?" she squealed.

No. No. No. It wasn't exciting, not in the slightest bit. Zed couldn't think of anything worse than having to stand up in front of a bunch of people and not only talk but have to act as well? He started to feel increasingly hot and his palms began to sweat in response to the dread that weighed heavily within the pit of his stomach. His breathing became shallow and his head felt dizzy;

internally he pleaded with her to choose anyone else other than him. He surveyed the room to establish how he could escape. A trip to the toilet perhaps? But he would still be faced with the same dilemma on his return... He had to get out of there before she asked him to read.

Q, stood up like a lightning bolt. *"They made the role of narrator for me!"* he sang while throwing his arms up in the air and giving the class a twirl. This caused the class chuckle; they were all so awed by him. Even Miss Kind gave him a knowing nod and smiled as she reminded him she had to give everybody an opportunity to audition for the part.

Zed was paralysed with fear; he had his face against his table, buried beneath a book. He knew that it did little to mask his presence, so he slid towards the ground and wrapped his head with his jumper. Hopefully, Miss Kind would choose everyone else to read first and then by the time she got to him, it would be lunchtime. That was his hope, but instead of being less visible, his decision to slip under the desk only caused Miss Kind to focus her attention on him.

What a curious thing to do. She thought. In all of her five years of teaching at Nerrison, she had never seen a child behave in that manner, and she didn't quite know what to do.

"Um... Zed? Everything okay under there? Have you dropped something?" She couldn't understand why he was behaving in such a peculiar fashion. "Come on now, get out from under there!" She repeated the instructions several times and received no response.

"Perhaps he is ill?" another student called out.

"Zed? Are you not feeling well?" Miss Kind asked.

All the other children looked at Miss Kind for some sort of explanation but unfortunately she was just as clueless as they were. The class moved their collective gaze from Zed (still under the table) to Miss Kind, who started to panic ever so slightly.

"Zed, sweetie, you are holding up the lesson and it's not fair to your classmates. Come on now, out from under there."

Miss Kind incorrectly assumed that Zed wanted the part of the narrator; she deduced that Q's confidence over the allocation roles had upset him.

"You can read first, Zed," she said.

That remark was more than Zed could handle; he became consumed with fear, which transformed into rage. The energy had nowhere to go other than outwards, and he exploded!

He propelled the table above his head, which went flying across the room with such force that it cracked as it smashed against the classroom wall. He picked up his chair and threw it against Miss Kind's computer which shattered her screen. Everyone gasped as they watched in terror, while Zed continued to bang, smash and crash his way around the classroom. He turned the class bookshelf upside down and emptied all the pencil pots onto the floor. In the midst of his fury, he also broke a desk and three chairs whilst screaming incoherently at Miss Kind and his peers. He knew what he was doing was wrong, but he couldn't help himself. He could see the horrified looks on everyone's faces and the utter panic in Miss Kind's eyes, as she ushered the children into the hallway and instructed Juno – a petite member of the athletics team – to rush to Mrs Long-Bottom's office for support.

This had happened before, many times, and Zed knew that he just needed to let the rage travel its course. After he had toppled the last table in the classroom, he finally reached the stage where he had burnt off some considerable energy and all that he could do was collapse into a heap in the centre of his destruction. Zed realised that he had acted irrationally, but he couldn't help it. He wished so much that he was just like the other kids that could talk about the things that worried him or just read as well as them. But he couldn't.

Zed ended up back in that place where he had been earlier in the day, in Mrs Long-bottom's office, but this time she was not smiling.

"Zed Brow!" Mrs Long-Bottom's voice resonated with an ear-shattering shrill. He winced, as he braced himself for the familiar monologue that every headteacher he had ever encountered had subjected him to.

"Your behaviour is worse than anything I have ever seen in my whole entire life," she seethed with a look of utter disgust on her shrivelled face. "I am going to call your parents. Stay in the hallway and do NOT move a muscle until I instruct you to do so!"

There was a remarkable contrast in her treatment of Zed from the welcoming introduction he had received at breaktime. Just as he predicted. Cast out from the 'family' even before lunchtime.

Feeling deflated, Zed retreated, out of Mrs Long-Bottom's office. He was used to being the outcast, but this definitely had to be a record. He wasn't worried about his parents being called. Not in the slightest bit. In fact, they didn't care much for him and cared even less about what he did. Oh, they would appear at school all right, pretend they were interested, perhaps even present themselves as being shocked and horrified by what he had done. But he knew that was all just for show. His mother and father didn't care what he got up to, not one dot.

Zed's mum was a 'collector' of sorts, or at least that's how she described it. Others, including his father, defined it as 'hoarding'.

His mother was fanatical about collecting. In fact, it was her full-time occupation. They were far from the richest family in the world and Mrs Brow was obsessed with finding something rare and wonderful that she could sell for a ridiculous sum of money.

Of course, she was still waiting to find that hidden gem but, until then, she promised herself not to let anything go to waste. Whatever she found, she kept.

On the way to school each morning, she had developed the routine of stopping off at the local recycling centre and filling up her car with 'treasures'. She liked to get there early in case someone else stumbled onto something valuable before she did.

That morning her finds included a chair with a missing leg, a cushion that was shaped like a pineapple and a full-length, broken mirror. It was quite ridiculous! The mirror was cracked from the top left-hand corner all the way down to the bottom right-hand corner. What would anyone possibly want with a semi-shattered mirror?

Zed's dad on the other hand was the complete opposite. He disliked mess or clutter. He was a minimalist and only owned one pair of shoes, one coat, one hat and one jumper. Mr Brow spent the majority of his life at the hospital where he worked as a porter, and he loved it. He probably worked so much so he could stay out of the house for extended periods of time. He rarely saw Zed and he hardly minded either.

Looking down at his wristwatch, Zed realised it was lunchtime, and he was absolutely starving.

"Hungry?" a voice boomed from above as though it had read his mind. Zed raised his head and met the gaze of a friendly, semi-familiar face towering above him.

"I know you!" Zed perked up.

"Really? I don't think we've been introduced. You're the new kid aren't you?"

"Sorry, I mean I saw you earlier, in the playground. Q and his friends pointed you out to me. To be completely honest, they actually warned me to stay away from you."

"Oh, is that so?" Hill's exaggerated tone of voice suggested that he wasn't in the least bit surprised by Zed's revelation and even less concerned with how others perceived him. "Then perhaps I should just take this delicious plate of steaming hot spaghetti back to the lunchroom then? You know, seeing as we are not supposed to be seen together?" Hill raised an eyebrow, as he attempted to turn away from Zed.

"No. No. Please don't!" Zed yelled as he reached out for Hill's arm, stopping him in his tracks. "I am really hungry. I haven't had anything to eat all day."

Hill turned towards Zed and smiled kindly.

"I was only messing with you. Actually, Miss Kind asked me to bring this to you," he whispered, offering the plate to Zed. "Doesn't your mum feed you then?"

Zed was too busy gulping down large forkfuls of pasta to reply. Hill stood in awe as he watched Zed shovelling food into his mouth with such speed, he barely had time to chew. Within moments the plate was completely clean; he even licked the sauce off the plate that his fork failed to scoop up.

Self-conscious about how quickly he had eaten, Zed looked up at Hill and apologised with his eyes. Hill tried to reassure Zed as he flashed him a smile. "There's nothing to be embarrassed about. I love my food too and hey, when you're hungry, you need to eat. Right?"

Despite his bully boy reputation, Hill was actually quite skilful at deducing what people were thinking and how they were feeling by picking up on their micro-expressions. It was like his superpower. At that moment, Hill sensed that Zed was uncomfortable with the topic of conversation and he swiftly changed tact.

"So, what's your name, new kid?"

Sensing an absence of judgement about his eating manners, Zed regained his dignity. He was thankful that the line of inquiry had moved on from why he hadn't eaten breakfast.

The truth was, he seldom had much of anything to eat. His mother spent not only a ridiculous length of time but also all her money on 'treasures' and his father was hardly ever home and when he was home he was in his room sleeping.

The one positive aspect of school for Zed was that he got a large (in his opinion) portion of hot food. Sometimes his school lunch was the only thing he would eat in a twenty-four-hour period.

Zed tucked the empty lunch plate under his seat, stood up and offered his right hand to Hill. "My name is Zed Brow." He smiled for the first time that day as he joked, "Perhaps I should have started with that introduction, but I've moved schools so many times, and maybe that's the reason why I don't really get to know people. You seem more genuine than most of the other characters I have met today though."

That was the first nice thing that any child had said to Hill at Nerrison. He was so used to being ignored, and Hill enjoyed talking to someone who didn't immediately assume he was scary. "That's nice of you to say. I'm sure you've heard that I have a reputation for being the school 'bully'? Well, that's not true. I've accepted it now though; I don't mind spending time alone during the day, it gives me plenty of time to think and I quite enjoy studying people. During the day I kind of store things up that I want to talk about, then I save them for when I get home and can share them with my mum. She is amazing. She always listens to me and has funny stories to tell me. It's just the two of us; she is my hero. I don't know what I would do without her."

Zed couldn't help but feel extremely envious of Hill. Even though Hill was an outcast at school (just like him), at least he had someone at home who loved and cared for him. Maybe Zed's parents loved him, but they certainly didn't care for him!

Zed's thoughts were interrupted when he heard the unmistakable 'clip-clop shuffle'. That's what he had nicknamed his mother's distinctive walk. She was absolutely obsessed with shoes – she had sixteen pairs at his last count – all high heels, and she did not know how to strut in them competently. She would step forward, one foot after the other and then drag her feet across the floor, whilst she steadied herself before mustering the confidence and energy to take two more steps.

With her trademark scarlet lip gloss and shoulder-length frizzy hair, she thought she was extremely elegant, but really it was quite embarrassing! Her motto was 'pretend you are astonishing and you will feel amazing!' Zed wasn't convinced, and he didn't think she had fooled anyone else either.

"Zed Brow!" she called out to him from the other end of the long passageway, huffing and puffing as though she had tried to run in those heels. Zed noticed that his father was shuffling his way down the hall right behind her. Oh dear, when both of his parents arrived at school that was an assured sign that he would definitely be excluded.

Zed turned to Hill and waved. "This means exclusion for certain. It was nice to meet you Hill."

Hill took that as his cue to leave and he whispered, "Good luck, man!" before disappearing back into the lunchroom.

Mrs Long-Bottom must have heard the clip-clop shuffle because she opened her office door, just as Mrs Brow arrived in front of it and lifted her fist to knock.

"Ah, Mr and Mrs Brow, I presume? Please do come in!" Mrs Long-Bottom was back to her welcoming cheery self; Zed found it hard to keep up with her mood. If only he could switch his feelings as quickly as that all his problems would be solved.

"Zed, you stay here while the grown-ups talk," she barked at Zed before smiling at his mother.

A short while later, the trio emerged from Mrs Long-Bottom's office. Clearly they found something amusing as they all chuckled on their exit.

"I can't apologize enough for our son's poor behaviour, Mrs Long-Bottom. It is such a wonderful school you have here, and we shall have some strong words with Zed tonight," Mrs Brow promised as she shot Zed a devastating look of disapproval.

"Come along, son," Mr Brow chipped in. "Home time for you, my boy."

Zed followed his parents out of the school, passed the car park, and they did not utter a word, so he did not say a word. Part of him was waiting to hear how disappointed they were with him. How he had let them down again; but nothing. Not a single comment. Zed secretly wished that they would tell him off, do something, anything.

But they didn't.

Home Sweet Home

Home was just a short fifteen-minute drive from the school but that was the longest fifteen minutes of Zed's life. Were they finally going to tell him off? Or inform him what they talked about with Mrs Long-Bottom? He was sure that they would be the first to break the awkward silence, even if it was only between themselves! Zed stood his ground and waited.

A painful fifteen and a half minutes later, they reached the place they called home (for that time). It was a thirteenth storey flat. The lift never worked, so Mrs Brow always took her heels off to climb the stairs. She did not have to put on a show for anyone, so she wasn't concerned about getting her feet dirty on the filthy concrete staircase. The journey up to the thirteenth floor was a challenge itself never mind with heels on. There was an overwhelming stench of rotting food that wafted up from the overflowing wheelie bins beneath the stairwell. The trick was to go up as quickly as possible. Even Mr Brow, who moved at a snail's pace on most occasions, developed a slight hop in his step when tackling the ascent.

They finally made it home and Mr Brow did what he always did when they arrived at their front door. First, he had to disengage the lock, which took some jiggling.

"We must get this fixed!" Mr Brow mumbled each time.

Entering the property was another challenge that got even more difficult with each passing day. The door's swing was restricted by books, magazines, cardboard boxes, clothes, bags, empty bottles, old maps, expired banknotes… you name it, they had it!

"Georgia Brow, if you keep filling up our flat with all this rubbish, there'll be no more room for us!" Mr Brow always complained to his wife, but it never made a difference. In fact, if anything it caused more harm than good. It terrified Mrs Brow that Mr Brow would reach a breaking point and throw out all her belongings. It made her findings even more precious to her.

"Jeffrey Brow!" she snapped. "One day we will be so rich and it will all be thanks to me. You need to support my passion and I promise you, it'll all be worth it in the end."

Zed rolled his eyes. He had heard that same conversation maybe a million times and nothing had changed. In all of his eleven years of life, she had been unsuccessful in her quest to find value in other people's rubbish, so why she thought it would ever happen was a mystery to both Zed and his father.

Still none the wiser about his fate, Zed probed his mother for answers, "So… What did Mrs Long-Bottom say?"

Mrs Brow looked at him as she mumbled, "No school tomorrow; surprise, surprise! Excluded for one and a half days, blah, blah. Go to your room!" She waved at him dismissively and turned her attention to her feet, which definitely needed a good scrub.

Zed knew better than to trouble them any more, so he retreated into his room. You wouldn't call it a bedroom… it had a mattress in it sure, but it also doubled up as a kitchen.

There was only one 'bedroom' in the flat and that belonged to his mother and father.

Zed's area was just as cluttered as every other place in the flat. He slept in a cosy spot, right next to the oven. His parents never cooked. They limited his range of meals to cereal, toast, the occasional microwave meal and if he was lucky, some seasoned chicken wings and chips. That was his absolute favourite! He usually had fiery wings and chips at the end of each month, when there was more disposable income. He didn't get fed that often at home, but when he did, it was a real treat. Perhaps that is what made the food taste so much better?

Zed crawled under the covers of his rollout mattress (that was always out) and picked up his pencil and doodle book that never left his room. Drawing… creating art, was the one thing that gave him the purest of pleasures and it was something that he wanted to keep to himself. Zed could create weird and wonderful creatures and to him they were real. In fact, he loved them as though they were his very best friends.

He attributed personalities, likes and dislikes to each character. He devoted more time to the characters in his book than he did to his parents. Oh, Zed would have preferred evenings talking to his parents, playing board games with them or watching television while commenting on the lives of others, but that was not his reality. His made-up world was important to him.

**

The next morning, Zed awoke to the sunlight from the kitchen window shining on his face. The boxes and bin liners full of bits and bobs stacked up around the room did a fair job of blocking most of the natural light, but a few stray rays of sun peered through.

Zed's stomach growled. The last meal he had eaten was the pasta at lunch the previous day. He poked around the kitchen to see if there was some cereal or bread, but there wasn't. He opened the fridge door hoping he would find some milk, but he didn't. In fact it had been so long since they had put anything in the fridge, it wasn't even switched on. Perhaps that was his parents' way of saving money. There's no point in cooling non-existent food.

Fighting his way into the living room over suitcases, black bags and boxes he called out to his parents.

"Mum? Dad? Is there anything for breakfast this morning? I'm starving!"

He waited for the usual dismissive comment; telling him to be quiet and to 'stop making a fuss,' but there was silence.

He probed for a response again.

"Hello?"

His dad responded by shouting from the bedroom. "Mum's left."

Zed didn't quite understand what that meant. Did it mean that his mum had gone out to get some food? He really hoped that's what his father had alluded to, but it was more likely that she had left early, for her routine trip to the recycling centre.

Confused and uncharacteristically optimistic, Zed prompted his dad for further clarification. "What do you mean she left, Dad? Is the car still here?"

Mr Brow appeared from his bedroom dressed in his work uniform.

"Just what I said," Mr Brow snapped, looking extremely irritated. "I'm not sure where she is, but I woke up at four a.m. to go to the toilet, and she wasn't there, so I assume that she took off in the middle of the night."

"Did she take the car?" Zed pushed for a direct response to his question.

"The car keys are still in my room on the dresser, so no."

Zed stood there open-mouthed. How could his father give him that news so matter-of-factly? Did he not care that his wife had fled without even an explanation? Where would she have gone at that time in the morning? Without the car?

"We'll be fine, kid," Mr Brow reassured him. "The plan now is to make this place look like a home. You don't have school today, so I want you to spend the day putting all the black bags and boxes out. All the odd bits and bobs need to be bagged and disposed of too. Okay?"

It was all happening so quickly. Zed did not want to be held responsible for throwing out his mother's possessions, without her permission. It was her worst fear! What if she walked back in whilst he was decluttering the place? It would not be very pleasant. Not for him at least.

In an attempt to change the subject, Zed asked about breakfast again. "Dad, I am really starving. I checked the kitchen and there's nothing in there."

"Oh, you are a fusspot!" his father retorted whilst rooting around under the living room settee cushions.

After a moment or two, Mr Brow pulled out a half-eaten chocolate bar, that was covered in dust and sofa fur. He gave it a short sharp blow, which did nothing to remove the dirt, and then offered it to Zed.

"Don't say I never give you anything," Mr Brow declared with a look of seriousness and a glint of sadness in his eyes. He knew that he could do better as a father, but he could not admit that to himself – never mind voice it out loud.

"I'm heading off now," Mr Brow continued, whilst gathering a few last-minute belongings from his room, for work. "It'll be another long day for me, so you will have plenty of time to get this place sorted before this evening. I would love to see the hallway carpet by the time I get home." He smiled gleefully at the anticipation of coming back to a clutter-free home.

Mr Brow's voice trailed off into the bedroom as he continued vocalizing his excitement. That was perhaps the most animated Zed had seen his father, well... ever.

Some people would think it somewhat strange to get excited about the thought of seeing carpeting, but not Mr Brow. Part of him had quite liked the fact that he would no longer have to live in disarray – or 'organized chaos' as Mrs Brow referred to it.

Left alone in the sitting room, Zed paused for a moment. He stared at the disturbingly appealing confectionery his father had handed him. His mind screamed at him, begging him not to put that filth into his mouth, but his tummy had other plans.

Removing the crinkled wrapper that enveloped a small portion of the chocolate bar, Zed devoured the whole thing, in two bites. It was disgusting... but it tasted so good!

Having temporarily tamed his stomach, Zed's mind drifted back to his mum. Could she have just disappeared without saying a word? She had never done anything like that before. It was extremely out of character. His mother lived by rigid routines, and she almost never deviated from them, unless she absolutely needed to for some unexpected reason.

Why was his father so unfazed by her disappearance? Perhaps he knew more than he had divulged? He had to!

Throughout the rest of the day, Zed spent his time sorting, stacking and binning a lot of bits and bobs. He worked tirelessly to declutter the flat and by four p.m. he had cleared the kitchen and the hallway. Zed was sure it would please his father and hoped that he would break tradition and treat him to some spicy chicken and chips as a celebratory treat. It wasn't quite the end of the month but the positive thought had kept Zed's energy levels just high enough to complete the task.

Feeling a sense of achievement, Zed felt like he deserved to put his feet up. There was a dining table that had been there when they first moved in, but it was only ever used as a storage device. As he took a seat at the table, Zed fantasized about having candlelit Christmas dinners with roast potatoes, brussel sprouts, nut roast, turkey, chicken, bacon, goose… food, food, food and more food.

As his mind wandered, Zed realised that his stomach had taken command of his thoughts again. The intense desire to eat something, anything, had taken over. A whole day had gone by and his tiny frame had been fuelled on nothing more than a grubby, half-eaten chocolate bar and a dream of some spicy chicken and chips.

Desperately trying to distract his thoughts, Zed peered out the kitchen window. The flat overlooked a playground and Zed watched on as his peers dumped their school bags on the tarmac and played without a care in the world.

He heard the echoes of laughter and gazed at the children with envy. He wished that he was carefree and could run around in the park, but his mother was not a huge fan of the outdoors and preferred for him to stay indoors where he was safe but out of her way. That was a significant contributing factor to him developing a love for art. Drawing was something that he could do, with very limited resources, and he didn't need to ask for permission to do it.

It dawned on Zed that his mum had disappeared and his dad was at work. It was a unique opportunity for him to do whatever he wanted. He contemplated going to the park to play with the other kids. There were two drawbacks to that plan: firstly it appeared that all the other boys knew each other, so he wouldn't have anyone to play with, and secondly, his stomach had sung that oh so familiar tune. He was weak and dizzy. He needed to eat something.

Zed knew it was pointless searching for food in the house. If there was anything to be found, he would have uncovered it whilst decluttering the flat. His best bet was to search for some money, so he could buy something from the shop.

Zed rooted around in the sofa, the one his father had discovered the chocolate bar in earlier. He didn't find any other food in there, but he sourced a few coins. He wasn't sure what he could get for that amount, but that didn't matter. Whatever he could purchase would be better than having nothing. Armed with his coins, Zed raced to the local shop.

Cost-Low was a small convenience store located right next door to his block of flats. It had a very limited stock because a new mega-market had recently opened a little further down the road and most people did their weekly shop there. Steadily losing loyal customers, Cost-Low was rapidly going out of business. Zed would have preferred the variety and range of food on offer at the mega-market, but he needed to conserve as much of his energy as possible, so he stopped off at Cost-Low instead.

Upon entering the shop, it was visibly more sparse than he remembered it being when he visited the week before.

A clerk sat behind the towering counter. Clearly bored, he tried to entertain himself by reading one of the magazines available for purchase in the store, but it didn't appear to sustain his attention and he flicked through the pages far too swiftly to take any information in. Even the glossy coloured pictures weren't enough to hold his interest for more than a second or two.

Zed didn't bother to greet the clerk and his presence in the shop was not acknowledged either. He perused the meagre shelves and the truth was, everything looked appealing to him. He settled on a pork pie that was nearing its best before date, a bag of salted crisps, and a chocolate milkshake. It was going to be a feast.

Scrambling in his pocket, whilst trying not to drop the produce, Zed approached the till and beamed with anticipation as he deposited the coins on the counter for the sales assistant to count.

Without giving eye contact the employee glanced at the coins and murmured. "That's not enough cash."

A little shocked and very disappointed, Zed unwittingly put on his puppy dog face, which would have affected anyone who looked at him causing them to feel empathy, but unfortunately for Zed, the worker didn't even glance up at him.

"So, what can I get with this amount?" Zed asked.

"Only one item. They are all on sale for the same price!" The clerk appeared to be annoyed at Zed's question. Surely working in a shop that people hardly ever visited, one would welcome the human interaction; not this guy.

After much pondering, Zed informed the sales assistant of his decision.

"I will take the chocolate milk."

"Yup," he responded, with a blank expression and monotone voice, failing to look at Zed again. "Put the other items back on the shelf before you leave."

After scooping the coins and depositing them into the till the clerk resumed his magazine flicking.

Deflated and despondent, Zed retreated to the back of the store. Clasping the pie and crisps in his hands had made him even more ravenous than he had been five minutes prior to entering the shop. Zed reached out to place the pastry back on the fridge shelf and his stomach growled at him in anger. He paused for a moment and then looked up at the clerk who was still very much engrossed in his page-turning routine.

Would the clerk even notice if he were to walk out of the shop with the items in hand? Zed was riddled with guilt for entertaining the notion.

Growing with ferocity, his stomach scratched and growled at him like a caged lion trying to escape from within his tiny frame. It was too much for Zed to handle. He quickly shoved the crisps and pie into his pockets and without looking up, he scurried towards the exit.

Once outside, he sprinted as though his life depended on it. He could feel the adrenaline coursing through his body, his heart racing faster than he had ever experienced! Zed kept reminding himself to continue breathing so he wouldn't collapse from the anxiety and panic that he felt. He raced down the road until he found himself at the local park.

Throwing himself on the first bench he could find, Zed gasped, whilst his heart threatened to burst out of his chest. Once he regained control of his breathing, Zed reached into his pockets and recovered what he perceived as treasure… sustenance!

He started with the salty crisps, popping the bag open with a tight grip. He continued to squeeze the packet until all the contents became crumbs. Zed tilted his head back, and emptied the crunchy snacks into his mouth, as though he were drinking water. The crisps caused his cheeks to swell, and he chomped ferociously, only pausing briefly and occasionally to mumble, "Mmmm." It was a great feeling.

After washing it all down with the chocolate milkshake, Zed set his sights upon the pork pie. He decided to savour every moment; he gazed upon it while salivating. The thought of eating food was almost as satisfying as consuming it. Almost.

He took a deep breath in and could pick out all of the different herbs and seasonings that went into creating that rich buttery snack.

He was poised and ready to take his first bite but was jolted back to reality when he heard a familiar tone. Paying closer attention to the sound he realised who it was.

"Zed! Hi! Fancy seeing you here." Hill's voice boomed, as he towered behind him. "Zed, I'd like you to meet my mum."

Zed, was torn between sinking his teeth into the pork pie and making polite conversation, but then he remembered how thoughtful and genuine Hill had been to him when they last met.

With that thought in mind, he lowered his pastry, stood up and extended his hand to offer her a handshake. "It's lovely to meet you, Mrs Hillson," he uttered with a gentle smile.

Her eyes were compassionate, so warming, and at that moment he realised why Hill adored his mother.

"Enough of the *Mrs Hillson*," she mocked him tenderly. "There's no need for formalities. Franky has had nothing but good things to say about you. So, I consider you a friend of the family and all of my friends call me Trisha. Got it?" Trisha smiled mischievously, which caused Zed to blush.

"Yes, Mrs... um I mean Trisha." Zed giggled coyly.

"Right. On to more pressing matters," Trisha continued, "What are you still doing out? And what have you got in your hand there? You'll ruin your supper!" she quipped.

"Actually, my parents are working late, so this is my dinner." Zed could only bear to tell a half-truth. It was too much for him to admit that his mother had abandoned him, his father didn't care and that they had left him alone in the house, without food.

"Oh, you poor dear," Trisha whispered, trying not to embarrass him with her sympathy. "I'll have no arguments; you're coming to dinner at ours. I've been cooking all day, there's too much for just us two," Trisha declared, gesturing between herself and her son.

Zed's eyes widened at the thought of eating a hot meal. His excitement was difficult to contain. He jumped and squealed with delight. "I would love to!... um… If you wouldn't mind?"

Hill rolled his eyes and chipped in, "Don't be silly. Mum and I always have loads of leftovers. You are more than welcome!"

Zed tucked the pork pie back into his pocket, as he traipsed behind Trisha and Hill. He decided to save it for another time. A day which unfortunately was inevitable for him when he wouldn't have a preferable offer of a steaming plate of food. Zed couldn't believe his luck. He was delighted that he had bumped into Hill.

The Hillson's Residence

Back at the Hillson's residence, which turned out to be a flat near his on the other side of the small park, Zed sat down to possibly… no, definitely, the most amount of cooked food he had ever seen at a dinner table at one time. There were some ingredients he didn't even know the name of like artichokes, avocados, asparagus, kimchi and pan-fried pork gyozas, but it all tasted magnificent. So great in fact, that he didn't let his embarrassment get in the way of him asking for second and third helpings.

Throughout the meal, Trisha continually reassured him, "You don't need to ask permission to eat. Please, help yourself to as much as you want."

Trisha was a huge fan of cooking programmes and she frequently purchased exotic ingredients. She had a talent for producing exquisite tasting dishes. Trisha never used recipes, she was a creative cook who could create magic in the kitchen using her home-crafted gift. She weighed all the elements with her eyes and added an ounce of love to everything she prepared, and Zed tasted her kindness in every mouthful he savoured.

After the banquet, they played a board game a concept he had only ever seen adverts on telly about but never experienced. Hill had to explain the rules a few times, but Zed didn't mind. He was just so pleased to be part of something which was real and engaging with people who asked him about his thoughts, wishes, likes and dislikes. It was alien to Zed, but definitely a life he could get used to.

Throughout the entire evening, Trisha was the perfect host

with her welcoming nature. For the very first time in his life, Zed understood the meaning of happiness. He had such a wonderful evening, so much so, that the hours rolled by and he didn't even realise how quickly time had lapsed.

After the food and games were finished Trisha pointed out that it was late and that his parents would be worried about him. "If you were my son, I would wonder where you were. Not that I am chasing you away. You are welcome anytime you know that. Would you like me to call your folks to come and pick you up, Zed?"

Panicked and flustered, Zed blurted, "No, no, that's okay. I'm only across the road. I'll be home in less than five minutes. Probably quicker than it would take for them to answer the phone." He smiled wearily, hoping he had said just enough to avoid suspicion.

Trisha examined him through squinted eyes, clearly weighing up the risk involved in allowing him to wander home alone in the dark. Zed widened his gaze, hoping to reassure Trisha whilst mentally pleading with her to let it go.

They both smiled at each other simultaneously. They had reached an agreement.

"Okay, Zed," she conceded. "I suppose you do only live a stone's throw away. Franky and I will stand out on our balcony and watch you enter your flat. That is not negotiable," she quipped with affection and settled with her trademark smile.

Zed was happy with that plan. He did, however, struggle to understand why she cared so much about someone she had only just met. His heart warmed and for the first time in a long while, he felt like he belonged.

Zed had overestimated how long it would take to get from Hill's home to his flat. In actual fact, it only took one hundred and twenty seconds from door to door. Winded from racing himself down (and then up) thirteen flights of stairs, Zed beamed with pride as he wiggled his key in the lock and waved a final goodbye to the Hillsons.

Upon entering his flat, it felt different. For a start, it was nice to come home to a clutter-free living space. He knew his dad wasn't home yet because Mr Brow finished work at nine p.m. and it took him at least twenty minutes to walk back from the hospital. Zed could do it in eight minutes and most other people could probably do it in eleven, but his father was someone who was never in a hurry, not even when he was late for something. Mr Brow was a man of few words. Perhaps it was because he spent so long doing everything. He would run out of day before he had a chance to talk about any of it.

Feeling full and utterly emotionally satisfied, Zed crawled into bed with a smile on his face and a little glow in his heart.

A Choice To Make

Zed woke up the next morning slightly later than usual, partly because he was out so late the evening before but mostly because he wasn't woken up by hunger pains. In fact, he was still pretty stuffed from the feast the night before. It was the best night's sleep he had ever had.

He bounced out of his roll away mattress and hurried into his parents' bedroom. Expecting to see his father still snoozing, as he pretty much always did, Zed only had to glance at the bed to realise something was peculiar. He noticed that the bed had been slept in as expected, but the strange thing was that it wasn't made up.

Mr Brow always made a habit of straightening the covers when he woke up each morning. It was the only control he had over the order in the family home. He could just about cope with what Mrs Brow considered to be 'organized chaos' as long as he had a clutter-free, tidy bed to sleep in each night. Mr Brow had a strict regime which involved tightly tucking his bedsheets under the mattress and fluffing the pillows. Perhaps he had relaxed the lifelong routine now that he didn't have to worry about keeping order in all the other rooms of the property? Zed thought that was an unlikely possibility.

Glancing at the antique clock on the bedside table, Zed realised that it was almost time for school. He began to panic; he felt his heart rate and body temperature rise... that was never a good sign. A dreaded thought entered his head and as incomprehensible as it seemed, Zed could not shake the notion.

Was it possible that his father could have just got up and left him in the middle of the night?

He scampered around the bedroom, searching desperately for clues, anything that would indicate where his father had gone. First, his mother disappeared without warning or a trace and now his father had vanished! *How was that possible?* People do not just evaporate into thin air – but that is exactly what had appeared to have happened to him, twice within the space of one week.

Zed had a choice to make. He could continue to attend Nerrison primary school and pretend as though nothing was wrong, or he could go to the police station and tell them everything… *Everything?*

More than likely, it could mean that police would inform social workers who would put him into the care system. He didn't much like the thought of living with strangers. Although a possible positive outcome would be that he got a fresh start, an opportunity to be looked after – properly cared for and cherished by someone just like Trisha adored Hill.

Zed sat slumped on the floor and tried to stifle his sobbing. He had never imagined that anything so devastating could happen to him. He was all alone in the world at that moment and wanted nothing more than for his parents to shuffle in through the front door and tell him he was overreacting and call him a 'fusspot'.

That never happened.

Savouring Every Meal

Over the following weeks, Zed formed his own unique routines and coping strategies. He woke up each morning and got ready, ensured he was on his best behaviour in school and worked incredibly hard to stay out of trouble, which took a significant amount of energy to achieve. Zed knew that if he was sent to Mrs Long-Bottom's office again, it would trigger a phone call home, and he could not have that. Zed protected his secret fiercely.

Most evenings he would visit Cost-Low on the way home from school, so he could pick-up some sustenance for dinner. It was usually something small, like a bag of sweets or a pork pie – that was the easiest item to select. The pies were home-made and wrapped in cling film, which didn't produce a rustling sound when he shoved it into his pocket. Although, even if he created the loudest racket in the shop, he was 99% sure that the despondent clerk wouldn't have noticed or cared.

Zed still felt a sense of crippling guilt every time he exited the shop with a pocket full of food. But, with limited options, he believed he had to steal in order to survive.

There were some days where Zed invited himself over to the Hillsons' flat. They were invariably welcoming on every occasion and, during their evenings together, they helped to create some of Zed's most memorable experiences – laughing and getting to know one another over each delectable feast.

If Zed had turned up at Hill's home every evening, they probably wouldn't have minded. The only thing that stopped him was the fact that he did not want them to ask probing questions about his parents' whereabouts.

Zed consistently used the excuse that his dad was working late and that his mother was away on business. He assumed that two evenings a week was probably a socially acceptable limit to be left alone. Not wishing to arouse suspicion, Zed decided that he would top-up his calorie intake with Cost-Low produce for the other five days of the week.

Both Trisha and Hill had grown quite fond of Zed and the feeling was most definitely mutual. Zed desperately looked forward to those cosy evenings in their home. Not just for the unique, satisfying dishes that Trisha served up each night, but also for their company. He hadn't fully realised just how lonely he was until he met them.

Hill treated Zed like the sibling he never had. They would talk for hours about the funny things that happened at school and they came up with some hilarious top-secret nicknames for all the teachers. At school, they always sat together at lunch and also during their Year six production rehearsals. Hill knew that Zed struggled with reading – only a few people did, as Zed hid it well – so Hill helped him practise for their weekly comprehension tests, and it helped him immensely!

Trisha was so thoughtful and gentle. She made sure that she took every opportunity to ask them how their day was; she was a firm believer in sharing feelings. Trisha regularly reminded them that, "Problems always seem bigger in your head than they actually are in reality." She also regularly stated that, "Life is better when you share." She practically sang those phrases pretty much every time they sat down to dinner together.

Mega Supermarket

It had been a month since Mr and Mrs Brow's disappearance and Zed planned to pick up his dinner as usual from Cost-Low, because he had eaten with the Hillson family the previous evening. The only problem was, he couldn't stand the thought of chomping into another gelatinous savoury pie.

On his walk home from school he took a detour and headed towards the giant supermarket to see what he could pillage from its shelves. He was extremely anxious about the thought of stealing from somewhere new, but somehow he managed to convince himself that it would be easier because there would be lots of families shopping in the after-school rush. He hoped that shoppers wouldn't notice him.

Zed had never been inside the giant supermarket before, but immediately after entering, he understood why people stopped shopping at Cost-Low. It was like crossing the threshold into a produce wonderland. There must have been at least one hundred aisles bursting with fresh fruit, and vegetables, canned meats, tinned goods and at least eight aisles dedicated to different cereals and grains.

Within the store, there was a fully stocked bakery, a deli counter, a fish stall and a confectionery stand. There was so much to choose from, Zed didn't know where to start.

Dazzled by the seemingly never-ending rows of food, Zed stumbled backwards into a shelf with cured meats, causing a few packets to fall to the ground and land at his feet. He ducked down to retrieve them and paused for a moment.

Before placing the packages back on the rack, he stealthily stuffed one into his pocket, successfully concealing the crime. Zed glanced around. As predicted, everyone else was preoccupied with their own shopping and he didn't notice any security guards anywhere.

Zed's heightened level of anxiety eased somewhat; he had convinced himself that no one was watching. He scurried around the aisles throwing whatever he could fit into his rapidly expanding pockets. *Why hadn't he thought about visiting the store before?* It was the perfect place to pick up whatever he craved. It was like being in a scrumptious playground where his only limitation was the dimensions of his clothing compartments.

Almost at capacity and feeling overloaded, Zed spotted the doughnut aisle. *Maybe he could discreetly conceal just one more item?* With no space left in any of his pockets, socks or trouser legs, Zed swiftly shoved some sugar-coated, jam doughnuts in between his shirt and his school jumper. He took extra care to ensure that he tucked his jumper into his trouser waistband so that the sugary snack wouldn't fall out.

With pockets stuffed to the brim and doughnuts nestled across his miniature frame, Zed finally conceded that he was over-encumbered and he waddled towards the automatic doors to exit the superstore.

Zed had successfully avoided all security guards in the shop. He took a final brief glance around and then he stepped out of the shop. Preoccupied with the overwhelming sense of relief he felt, Zed failed to focus his attention on his path ahead and he bumped into a burly, angry-looking woman. They collided with such force it caused the bag of doughnuts to pop open and the red, sticky jam oozed down his shirt. The jumper concealed the gooey mess, but that was the least of his worries.

With his head down and slightly distracted, Zed stepped to the left, to get out of the lady's way, but she intentionally took a step right, and she was smack bang in front of him again. He repeated the action, this time mumbling, "I'm sorry. Excuse me." But the same thing happened again.

What was the lady doing? Zed looked up and upon closer inspection, she was furious. He could tell because her teeth were gritted her nostrils flared, and she had beads of sweat dripping down from her hairline past her ears that had an earpiece attached... an earpiece! *It couldn't be. Could it? Was she... actually a security guard?*

Zed swallowed hard, as he stared into the fury plastered across her face. He studied her, anxiously waiting for her to give some insight into her identity.

She grabbed him by the arm, lifting his tiny frame a few centimetres off the ground and dragged him back through the automatic doors.

"You're coming with me!" she bellowed with a thunderous tone.

The woman escorted Zed to what could have been described as a holding cell. It was a tiny basement without windows or natural light. The beige room was dimly lit with a flickering desk lamp that unsettled him. There was a single wooden table which had two foldable chairs on either side.

It seemed bizarre that the superstore would need such an oppressive space. Zed was convinced that they created the cubicle for precisely that purpose – to terrify and intimidate any apprehended shoplifters.

As the gravity of the situation began to sink in, Zed couldn't help but panic about what would happen to him. He heard mutterings outside the door shortly after the security guard had thrown him into the room. There were whispers about informing the police and his parents. His world was about to come crumbling in once more and so soon after his parents had abandoned him.

Zed waited for what seemed like hours in the chamber and then he heard the jiggling of the door handle. Exhausted and slumped across the table, Zed bolted upright in his seat. A fresh wave of fright took over him; he felt the sweltering heat of anxiety course through his body.

Two male police officers entered the room first, and they were closely followed by a female with a jacket embossed with 'Manager' across the top pocket and a slender woman, who wore a petite trouser suit and somehow reminded him of Miss Kind. Perhaps it was the perkiness in her step or the tireless grin on her face. Whatever it was, Zed drew comfort from it.

The petite lady with the warm eyes was the first to speak. She sat across the table from Zed and studied him, whilst expressing concern and empathy for him. "Hello, young man," she whispered as she leaned in. "My name is Monica and I'm a social worker." Monica could see the alarm spread across Zed's face as his gaze widened.

"Oh please don't worry," she continued softly. "I've been made aware that you took some things out of the shop without paying. The police are just here as a precaution. What's your name?"

Zed didn't know whether to tell her everything? Nothing? Or maybe just some half-truths? He was becoming quite good at sharing partial lies now; similar enough to the truth so he could remember what he had said, but not too close to the truth, as that could result in him going into the social care system, or worse getting arrested!

After weighing up his options, he decided to stick to partial-truths. He explained that his name was Zed (correct).

It was his first offence (partly true). It was the first time he had stolen from the megastore and the first time anyone had caught him.

As for why he stole? Well, he played it down and said, "I was just bored and did it for a laugh." Well… that was definitely a lie.

Then there was the big one. The whopper… He said that Trisha was his aunt, and he was staying with her while his parents were away on a business trip. That was definitely not true!

The store manager agreed not to take the case any further and requested that the police give him a warning. This consisted of an intense forty-five-minute talk on the dangerous path he was skirting on and a caution outlining that if he continued to steal he would end up in prison.

Zed listened intently for the duration of the lecture and then fell apart. He realised his body was burning up, as sweat trickled down his face. Zed's breathing quickened, and he sobbed into his school jumper. Zed felt a wash of exhausting emotions – guilty, ashamed, abandoned and terrified simultaneously. If he thought he had any other viable option other than stealing, he would have taken it.

Satisfied that Zed had been appropriately reprimanded, the police retrieved all the stolen items and agreed that the issue was resolved and the matter was closed. The social worker, however, insisted on escorting him 'home'. *There was no way that he could half-truth his way out of that.*

No Turning Back

Zed led Monica, the social worker, towards Franky Hillson's flat. There was no way he could have taken her to his place. He knew that she would have rumbled him instantly. Firstly, Monica was a trained professional, and it was highly doubtful that he would have satisfied her inquiring mind with the lie about his parents being away on a business trip. He had told that story to Hill and Tricia on more than a few occasions.

Secondly, the narrative he created about shoplifting out of boredom, would have been exposed as untrue if Monica was the snooping kind – which he figured she was.

A sinking feeling washed over Zed. He visualized Monica with an accusatory, furrowed brow and mouth agape, as she peered inside his empty kitchen cupboards, exposing him as the liar he was.

The fact that his fridge wasn't even plugged in would also signal alarm bells. No… There were just too many questions that he wouldn't be able to provide suitable answers to.

His best bet was to lead Monica to Hill's flat and hope that Hill answered the door. Zed assumed that he was the most likely resident out of the two who would support the stories he had told Monica.

After pressing the doorbell, Zed held his breath in silent prayer as they waited outside the Hillson residence. Monica hummed softly to herself, completely oblivious to Zed's internal anguish.

Moments later – although it felt like an age to Zed – the door eventually swung open and Zed's hopeful heart sank. Usually, her cheery grin was the highlight of his week, but not today.

Trisha's expression swiftly evolved from her usual infectious smile to a look of concern. She instinctively knew that the woman with Zed was not his mother. Firstly, she was missing a trademark scarlet lip gloss that Zed had mentioned on a few occasions and secondly, and most importantly, Zed grimaced as though he were bracing himself for an onslaught of some description.

Trisha reached out for Zed and placed a protective arm around him. "Hiya, Love," she gently greeted him. Trisha often referred to him as 'Love'. She saw him as a second son and treated him as such.

Concerned for his well-being, Tricia's maternal instincts took over. She instinctively knew that Zed was petrified and although she didn't know what he was so fearful of, she felt that it was her duty to reassure and comfort him.

Trisha crouched down as she reached out for Zed, drew him closer, and placed a protective arm around him.

Overwhelmed with emotion, Zed began to sob. "I'm very sorry, Trisha. I'm so, just so sorry." Those were the only words he could string together before succumbing to the warm tears that streamed down his rosy cheeks.

Trisha pulled him in closer and reassured him. "It's okay, Love. Whatever it is, we'll sort it. It can't be that bad? You're here and you're safe with me. It's all right."

Trisha looked up expectantly at Monica from her crouched position as she waited to be filled in.

Monica was humbled and slightly distracted by the display of love and affection between the two of them. In her job she had seen a vast spectrum of relationships and scenes like that were her favourite. It was exactly why she had decided to become a social worker in the first place – to support loving families.

Monica snapped back to reality and introduced herself. She explained that Zed was caught shoplifting and even though the police were called, everyone had agreed that Zed was remorseful and unlikely to do it again.

Trisha did not react with shock. She turned to Zed and offered him additional comforting assurances.

"Zed. It's okay," she whispered sweetly. "I know everything now and the world hasn't ended. So, you made a mistake. Who hasn't?" She chuckled. "Remember last week when I got all the way to the school gates before I realised I had my T-shirt on backwards, and I still had my fluffy slippers on?" They both smiled, which helped to lighten the mood.

"And even then, you only noticed when you stepped in a puddle," Zed added with a giggle.

"**Rookie error!**" They roared in sync.

They had laughed about that incident a few times since it happened.

Content with the outcome of her involvement in the case, Monica knew that Zed was in good company. She observed a strong bond between the pair and took that as her cue to take off.

"Mrs Hillson, I will leave Zed in your care. He is so lucky to have you. What a wonderful aunt you are." Monica left them embracing, and she was content that she had done her job effectively.

"Aunt?" Trisha looked up confused, but Monica had already begun her descent to the ground floor.

No More Half-truths

Zed, Trisha and Hill sat down to their regular weekday feast. Zed looked at his best friend who was oblivious to the events that had unfolded earlier with the police and social worker. Hill had been at his usual Friday night scouts club.

In Hill's absence, Trisha had promised Zed that she wouldn't tell anyone about his stealing. She said, "Nobody deserves to have their mistakes thrown back in their face once they'd owned up and taken responsibility for their actions." She told him she would never talk about it again unless he brought up the subject.

Zed reflected on how Trisha handled the situation: with love, understanding and compassion. He realised that he could tell her anything, and he kicked himself for not acknowledging it sooner.

Zed placed his cutlery down beside the mountain of food on his plate. "Hill?" he began, "There's something you need to know." Zed turned to Trisha and continued, "I'm sorry. I've not been entirely honest with you either."

Zed had held it all in for so long and when he started talking, he couldn't stop. He told them both how he was ignored/invisible for most of his life and explained that his mother was a hoarder and was obsessed with trying to get rich. He revealed that he had been living alone for the past month since the disappearance of his parents and finally admitted that he had shoplifted to survive, and the only reason he believed he got caught was because he became tired with the monotony of eating pork pies and crisps.

An overwhelming sense of relief washed over Zed after the unburdening of his conscience. Hill was glued to his seat, awestruck and unable to utter a word. It was a considerable amount to process. How could they have spent so much time together, and yet Hill didn't have a clue that his friend was suffering under the immense pressure to survive alone?

Hill's thoughts took him through a rollercoaster of emotions starting with a wave of sadness for his dear friend and a slight twinge of anger and resentment. He had told Zed absolutely everything about himself; he was an open book, but Zed hadn't trusted him with the truth. The emotional ride finally parked at compassion – Hill took solace in his mother's response to Zed's revelations.

She softly affirmed: "I'm glad that you were comfortable enough to tell us Zed. You've been so brave for so long, Love, but you're not alone. You can stay with us. We will look after you, won't we, Franky?"

Zed couldn't have hoped for a better response. Living with the Hillsons was more than he thought he deserved, but it felt like home.

***

After dinner, Trisha retreated to bed. It had been an incredibly long day for her, and she had promised the boys that they would head over to Zed's flat in the morning to help him retrieve his belongings and search the property for any clues linked to Mr and Mrs Brow's disappearance.

They all agreed that it was a good plan but left alone to ponder, Zed was desperate for answers. For so long, his thoughts were dominated by foraging for his next meal trying not to get caught stealing, as well as concealing the fact that he was living without adult supervision. Now that those issues were no longer pressing concerns, his new priority became to find his parents.

Zed convinced his trusted friend to go to his flat with him. Hill was always up for an adventure and as it had been Zed who suggested it, there was no way that he would let him down. Certainly not after everything he had heard that evening.

***

Back at Zed's flat, the lights were still working. The electricity hadn't been turned off from the mains by the energy company, even though the bill had been overdue for at least two weeks.

"We'll start off in Mum and Dad's bedroom," Zed said. He was sure that if they were to find anything out of the ordinary, it would definitely be in their room. He hadn't been in there since the morning of his father's disappearance and he hadn't seen Mr Brow since the day he gave Zed that last chocolate bar.

Zed pondered on that for a moment. He missed his father terribly. Even though he was a man of very few words – some words were better than no words at all. Mr Brow's presence comforted Zed; he missed the security of knowing where his parents were.

Everything seemed just as they had left it. Mrs Brow's eyelash curlers were still on her dressing stand and her hand cream was on the bedside table with the lid off. The (cracked) mirror that Mrs Brow had found on her last known trip to the recycling centre, had the pride of place opposite the bed.

"Nothing strange in here," Zed concluded as he slumped himself at the foot of the bed.

"Well, at least we tried," Hill added. "I'll be honest with you, Zed, it was a bit of a long shot." Hill offered Zed a sympathetic look, before slouching on the floor next to him. "Do you think we should head back now? I know it's Saturday tomorrow, but we are due back here early in the morning."

Zed conceded. He turned to the bed frame behind him to support his transition from sitting to standing and in doing so, he spotted something. Maintaining his crouched position, he glared for a moment.

"Hang on!" he called out to his companion.

Zed reached down under the bed and poking out from the shadows beneath the duvet, was a pair of male loafers. They were the loafers that his dad wore to the hospital, his work shoes. Zed knew for a fact that his father only had one pair. They were perfectly buffed and polished. This was another one of his father's routines he engaged in each evening before placing them in exactly that location.

It didn't make sense! Why were the loafers still in the flat? That would mean one of two things. Mr Brow had bought another pair. That was unlikely because he only ever bought a new pair of loafers once a year. Mr Brow typically celebrated the annual event by sleeping in his new shoes to 'break them in'. Zed would have remembered that. The only other explanation was that Mr Brow had left the flat without shoes on. That, however, seemed less likely.

"I just don't get it, Hill," Zed stressed.

"Maybe he wandered out in some slippers?" Hill offered as a suggestion.

Zed rushed to his parents' closet and, to his bafflement, his dad's single pair of house shoes were on the bottom rung of the wardrobe shelf, just as they had been every night before Mr Brow got home from work. As part of his routine, he would swap from loafers to slippers after his evening bath, and then he would place them back in the same location two minutes before bedtime and there they would remain until the following night.

"So, let me get this straight," Hill said as he attempted to process the information. "Your dad only owns two pairs of footwear. Work shoes – currently under his bed – and evening slippers, that are still in his wardrobe. Is that right?"

Zed struggled to accept the truth but agreed reluctantly. "Yes. That is right... but I don't know how that is possible. It just doesn't add up!" Zed stressed. He paused for a moment before continuing, "There is definitely something strange here. I think we might find out more if we stick around. I'd like to sleep in this room tonight."

Hill was unsure and worried about how his mum would react to him staying out all night, even if it was only across the road. The problem was that he didn't say where they were going. "I honestly don't think that's a good idea, Zed. It is getting kind of late; we should head back to mine."

"Oh, come on, Hill," Zed begged his friend. "We are just across the road, and we'll be back before your mum even gets up. What is the worst that can happen?"

Hill, unconvinced with the plan, still had his reservations.

"What if she wakes up to check on us tonight?"

"Does your mum often check on you in the night like a toddler?" Zed teased.

"No. I guess not. She's a deep sleeper. If anything, I'm more likely to get up in the middle of the night, than she is. Sometimes I go to the kitchen for a midnight snack – it's usually something leftover from dinner that I get a craving for... Yum, like those herby roast potatoes this evening; they were delicious!" Hill had gone off-topic, but Zed didn't mind. It was a sign that he was warming to the idea.

Zed gazed at his friend with a quizzical smile. "So... are we on?"

Hill smiled hesitantly, and replied, "We're on!"

Bedtime

The pair made a camp in Mr and Mrs Brow's bedroom – it was quite comfortable in there. Zed wondered why he hadn't swapped his rollout single bed in the kitchen for his parent's room sooner. There were rope lights draped over the interior bedroom windows which created a cosy Santa's grotto-like feel all year round. The walls were dressed in a brown and beige zebra print. The texture was reminiscent of the animal if you trailed your hands across it. The room looked like they had pulled it straight out of a double-page spread of an old glossy magazine, with no modern twists; Mrs Brow had an opulent, yet dated sense of style. Zed opted to sleep on the plush shag pile carpet that was so thick, it buried his hand right up to his wrist as he snuggled in for the night. Hill, however, preferred the solid double mattress on the bed. They both fell asleep as soon as they lay down.

***

In the early hours of the next morning, a piercing illumination sliced through the darkened room. Hill was the first to wake up; he was a light sleeper, by his own admission, and was irritated by the radiance, even though his head was buried firmly under the duvet.

"Turn the light off!" he snapped at Zed, squinting as he poked his head out from beneath the covers.

His friend didn't respond, so he tried again with growing impatience. "Zed! I'm trying to sleep."

54

Hill called out with a forceful, growling timbre to his voice. It caused Zed to bolt up from his slumber. Dazed and confused, Zed peeled one eye open, in an attempt to figure out why his friend was uncharacteristically annoyed.

The source of light summoned his attention; the rays perforated through the cracked mirror – the one that his mother had picked up from the recycling centre the day that she disappeared. Zed rubbed his eyes to check he was awake. Still uncertain, he crawled into the bed.

"Hill!" Zed whispered as he shook him rigorously.

"What?" Hill mumbled from beneath the duvet, which he had once again draped over his head.

"Do you see that?" Zed urged him. "Look!"

Hill reluctantly peeled the covers off his upper body and briefly peeped at his friend through one eye before closing it again.

"Is something wrong?" Hill sighed.

"Yes!" Zed shouted. The shock of Zed's raised voice caused him to take notice, and he scrambled out of the bed as though he had been electrocuted.

Hill scanned the room for less than a second before he zoned in on the mirror. "What… in… the… world?... That wasn't there when we fell asleep."

The pair stared at each other.

There was no way they were going back to sleep. Far too much adrenaline flowed through their veins.

For Hill, intrigue tipped the balance between fright and curiosity. He tiptoed towards the source.

"Wait. Stop! What are you doing?" Zed rebuked his friend.

"What's the worst that could happen?" Hill teased, failing to reassure his companion.

"I'm not sure, and that's the problem. We don't know what it is."

Hill ignored Zed's warning and headed towards the light, whilst his friend recoiled in horror. He reached out to touch the crack whilst leaning in for a closer inspection.

"Wow!... Come, see this!" Hill rejoiced. "There's something here."

Frozen with fear, Zed couldn't speak. His mind was screaming at Hill to retreat back into the bed. The duvet provided a sense of safety and normality. He struggled to process the events that were unfolding. The most movement he could muster was a slow-motion head shake.

Oblivious to Zed's internal hysteria, Hill touched the crack in the mirror and his finger entered through, uninjured by the glass. He sensed a cold darkness surrounding his finger. Hill was invited by the glow and a display of dazzling lights that danced across the surface of the mirror. He reached further in. This time his whole forearm was engulfed.

The crack widened as its beckoning intensified. The glass morphed into a shimmering black ink, still held perfectly in place by the bronze frame of the ornate vintage mirror. Without even a second glance, Hill vanished into the gooey gunk.

The shock of Hill's disappearance jolted Zed's body into action. He bolted from the bed and crept closer to the mirror. He half expected Hill to jump back into the room – but he didn't.

The rippled liquid slowed as its jelly-like consistency began to solidify from the top and crept its way down the mirror. Zed could tell that he was running out of time. He could either stand there and hope that Hill would spring back out of the mirror – which was increasingly unlikely – or, he could go in after him. He did not like the idea of leaping into the unknown. Not one bit.

His mind was flooded with images of Hill helping him with test preparation, sitting around his cosy dining table and laughing and joking with Trisha. God, Trisha. She would never forgive Zed if he let anything bad happen to her dear son.

With that last thought in the driving seat of his emotions, Zed crouched down beneath the mirror, pinched his nostrils together and forward rolled into the abyss.

Mirage

A shadowy veil shrouded the room, which concealed the answers to a thousand questions yet unasked. Disoriented, groggy and battered from what felt like an enormous drop from a never-ending spiralled staircase – with each step kicking him along the way – Zed winced as he surveyed the surrounding space for his friend.

"Hill? Are you in here, Hill?" he shouted, before pausing as he tensed to hear whether his call would be returned. There was no response.

Zed fumbled about in the darkness until he managed to steady himself onto his feet. His pupils dilated as they adjusted to the insufficient lighting, slowly piecing together a clearer picture of his surroundings. He was no longer within the safe confines of his parents' bedroom; he stood in the centre of what he could only describe as a glass cube. The mirror had entombed him.

Zed extended his arms to prevent himself from bumping into anything that could further injure his already fragile, bruised frame. He fumbled around, searching for a clue that would give him some indication of where his companion had gone.

"Hill!" he called. "Are you in here?"

Once again, there was no reply.

Overwhelmed with despair, Zed continued to clamour around the space, searching for his friend.

"You must be in here somewhere," he stated, vocalizing his thoughts. "I came in right after you! Where did you go?... Hill?...

Where are you?"

Exhausted and none the wiser, Zed collapsed into a heap on the floor, buried his head into his hands and wondered how he had arrived at that point.

In a matter of weeks, Zed had gone from spending most of his day alone in the cluttered kitchen he regarded as his safe space, to a completely alien environment. More than anything, Zed wished he could go back to the time when all he had to worry about was where his next meal was coming from.

He felt ill-prepared for this moment of debilitating dread and isolation. His sensitivity to loneliness had intensified after experiencing what it was like to live in a home filled with love and laughter. Trisha and Hill had done that for him. They had changed his life for the better, in ways that he never could have imagined.

A murmur infiltrated Zed's melancholy; it emanated from a corner of the cube. Steadying himself – both emotionally and physically – Zed made his way across the cold mirrored flooring, which was extremely unsettling. He wasn't sure how solid the ground was beneath him.

The room was not particularly large, but it took him longer than it should have to reach the other side as he deliberated every step. Ten confident strides would have achieved the same result more efficiently.

Hill awoke, still dazed, to an enthusiastic Zed, who shook him vigorously.

"I can't believe I found you, Hill. I thought I'd lost you forever."

Hill took a brief pause to compose himself. For a fleeting second, he had forgotten how he ended up in that room.

Reality crept back and sank in for Hill. Panic swept across

his expression, which unnerved Zed. He had never seen his friend display such a look of terror.

"What have I done?" Hill berated himself, covering his face with his hands. "This is all my fault! I brought us here. That was the dumbest decision I have EVER made!" Hill struck his forehead with open palms repeatedly.

Seeking to reassure him, Zed grabbed Hill's enormous hands to stop him from hurting himself. "It's okay, Hill. The good thing is that we are together. When I first woke up here, I thought I had lost you!"

Hill offered a half-smile. Even though they were trapped, Zed took comfort in the fact that they were a team.

"So, what do we do now?" Hill asked.

"Well, I guess another silver lining is we know what happened to my parents. They must have come in through the mirror during the night, just like we did. That's why Dad's shoes were still in the flat!"

Feeling less optimistic than Zed, Hill pondered for a moment. "How does that help us? We are trapped in here and I don't see them anywhere... Do you?"

"No... No. I don't," Zed conceded. "But they must be in here somewhere. I didn't notice you when I first woke up, but I found you! Perhaps there's a door, a window, or some way of getting out of here."

The pair scanned the room, but all they saw were mirrors beneath, beside them and above their heads. Zed leapt to his feet and thrust himself against all the surfaces thumping furiously, but not one of them shifted. Hill joined in, and used his weight against the walls, roaring, determined to shatter the glass. His efforts were also fruitless.

Frustrated and exhausted, they realised that if they were

going to make it out of the cube, then they would have to think creatively because, clearly, they would never break their way out of the place. The room had them trapped until they could figure out how to unlock it.

Hill slumped himself into a corner, whilst Zed stood in the centre of the room and once again inspected his surroundings. The only thing he could see was his reflection in front of him. He glanced to his left and noticed that there was no image. He then diverted his gaze to the right and there was also a reflectionless mirror.

"Hill?" he called out to his friend. "I think I've found something. Come and stand here."

Intrigued by the possibility of a lead, Hill shot across the room to where Zed was standing.

"What is it?" he urged, tracking Zed's eye-line to the image in front of them.

"What do you notice?" Zed asked, pointing forward.

"Um, your reflection?" Hill tentatively affirmed, whilst simultaneously querying whether it was a trick question.

"Do you have one?" Zed asked, barely moving.

"NO! No. I don't," Hill gasped as he glanced up, left and right, searching for his image.

"What does this mean? Am I not really here? What is going on?"

"And there's more," Zed added. "Take a closer look. None of the other mirrors have a reflection of *me* in them. Only this one." He gestured towards the figure that replicated his movements.

The pair stared at each other. Their minds were completely in sync. they decided to inspect Zed's reflection further. They cautiously tiptoed towards the mirror in front of them.

The image resembled Zed, but there were some subtle differences. The figure that stood before them was slightly taller than Zed. The eyebrows were a little fuller than his, but the most noticeable difference was the figure's blond rather than auburn hair colour. It wasn't obvious, but on closer inspection, it was definitely different.

Hill offered an explanation. "Maybe it's one of the magic mirrors that you find at the circus. You know them… The ones that can make you look really tall or super-wide… A distorting mirror. That's it!"

"Um… I'm not sure," Zed argued. "Have you ever seen a mirror that changes the shade of your hair?"

"I can't claim that I have, but this is all very strange to me. I can't say that I have ever been trapped in a mirror before either," Hill teased, for the first time since they had stepped through the mirror. His humour breathed an air of normality to an unusual situation and it was a comfort to them both.

Zed engaged with his reflection. He raised his right hand and, sure enough, the image responded as it was supposed to. He poked out his tongue, and it mimicked the movement. Every gesture was completely in sync, but Zed was still unconvinced.

There was an unfamiliar glare. Its eyes were pools of darkness.

"Who *are* you?" Zed called out.

"Who are *you?*" The mimic retorted in an echo-like voice.

Zed and Hill inhaled as they stood closer together. It became quite clear to the duo that the image was not Zed at all, but rather a completely different being entirely that had manifested itself as a replica of Zed.

Zed assumed that the way out of the mirror would be through interaction with the image. Hill came to the same conclusion as he murmured to his companion, "Maybe *it* knows what happened to your parents?"

"I expect this is our ticket out of here too," Zed whispered excitedly.

Once again, they turned to the thing and Zed asked, "Have you seen my mother and father? We think they might have gotten trapped in here somehow."

"I may have!" the creature snapped. It was visibly annoyed.

The boys were unsure of what to make from the response they were given, so Zed pressed. "Was that a yes or a no then? I guess my mum would have come in alone, followed by my dad on a different night?"

"*Maybe*," the mirror repeated, quite abruptly.

Zed didn't understand why the creature was being so impatient with him. All he had done was to ask whether it had seen his parents... Lost for words, his jaw dropped. It stumped him.

Being the expert in the art of communication of the pair, Hill stepped in to rescue the conversation. He decided to try a different tact because he believed that he and Zed had annoyed the creature, by gossiping to one another – something that his mother had always told him was unpleasant.

In a bid to cheer the being up, Hill smiled and offered an apology. "I am so sorry. I know that we were incredibly rude earlier whispering between ourselves. My mum raised me better than that. Please allow us to reset and start again?... Hello!"

The creature warmed to Hill and cracked a smile. It had clearly broken free from having to imitate all of Zed's movements and it morphed into something else. The image became fuzzy; its limbs evaporated, and it took on the shape of a green cloud with a void for a mouth and no other facial features.

"I am Hill and this is my very good friend Zed. What's your name?"

The figure dropped the Zed-like echo tone and responded in a deeper, chipper expression. "Well, hello there. I am Artichoke and I thought you would never ask. Forgive my irritation, I live a very lonely existence and I have always appreciated when people stop to take a moment to talk to me... I typically hear all the boring questions like, 'How did I arrive here? How do I get out? What is this place?' I have heard it all." Artichoke appeared to be mocking those who had entered the mirror before them and continued, notably pleased to be engaging in conversation for the first time in a long while. It turned into more of a monologue rather than a dialogue, but the duo understood why it was important to allow Artichoke to vent.

After hearing Artichoke's explanation of why it was upset, Zed understood and felt the need to echo Hill's apology. "I'm sorry for jumping in to ask you questions. That was rude of me and I have learned a lesson from it."

"That's okay," Artichoke replied, "All is forgotten. It is my duty to be the gatekeeper of Mirror Maze Land. I can delve into your psyche to figure out the best way to get your attention. Being a shape-shifter, I presented myself as your reflection. I knew it wouldn't take you long to notice the subtle differences between us. You see, the first law of being the gatekeeper is that I must not initiate contact with anyone. They have to acknowledge me before we can converse. Over the years I have developed ways to prompt people to communicate with me sooner rather than later – hence the use of costume," Artichoke concluded with a gracious nod, clearly quite pleased with itself.

Further enlightened, Zed and Hill repeated, "Mirror Maze Land!" simultaneously. That's where they were!

Hill felt like it was an appropriate time to explain how they ended up in Mirror Maze Land and how desperate they were to find Zed's parents and return home before morning. He described how caring and gentle his mother was and how frantic she would be if she woke up to discover them both gone.

"Both of us?" Zed asked Hill.

"Yes. Both of us, not just me. You are part of the family now. You are like a brother to me, and like it or not, my mum has promised to take care of you and to protect you."

Zed's heart warmed every time Hill and Trisha expressed love or concern for him. With each touching reminder, they showed him he felt more and more valued. He smiled to himself.

"Look… I am not unsympathetic, despite how I may come across," Artichoke started again and Zed and Hill secretly hoped that the shape-shifter wouldn't launch into another long monologue, but they courteously listened intently. "I know that you care deeply about your loved ones and you are both quite keen to get home safely, so here's the deal – please remember I do not make up the rules here. You can ask me one question between you and I will be completely honest in my response."

The boys widened their eyes… They could ask one question, but the trouble was, they had two questions!

"Is it okay if we have a chat to figure out what we would like to ask?" Hill requested.

"Yes… And there's your honest answer to your query used up. That was easy," Artichoke quipped with a smirk.

Zed and Hill gawked at each other.

"Are you serious? That was our one question done with?" Zed retorted in utter disbelief.

There was a pause which lasted several seconds, but felt like an hour…

"Nah, I'm just joking with you both. It's not often that I get to joke around. I'm sorry. Go ahead… Go. Have a discussion about what you wish to ask me." Artichoke could barely speak through its bellowing laughter. It clearly found its jokes more hilarious than Zed and Hill did.

Zed rolled his eyes in feigned amusement. He didn't want to do anything to annoy Artichoke again that could result in him being trapped in Mirror Maze Land for eternity. He definitely had no desire to do that!

Zed beckoned Hill closer and muttered, "So, what are we going to do, Hill?"

"I think we only have one choice here, Zed. We have to ask Artichoke how we can find your mum and dad."

"What? Wait! What about Tricia? We need to make sure that we get back before she sees our empty beds. I hate to say this Hill, but there is a risk that we may never get out of here," Zed warned.

"The plan can be both," Hill clarified. "We have come this far and it would be such a shame to head back without investigating what happened to your parents. They might be trapped somewhere and this could be our one and only opportunity to save them. So, here's what we do: We ask Artichoke to find them and then, we will figure out a strategy to get us out of here. All of us."

"I'm in," Zed confirmed. He didn't need much persuading to back the idea. It seemed like the only logical approach forward. Zed hated the thought of his parents being trapped somewhere, probably helpless and desperate for someone to rescue them. Hill had planted the image in Zed's mind and now that was all he could think about.

The duo gave each other a determined nod, before turning to

66

face Artichoke once again, who had been amusing itself by humming whimsically, pretending not to listen to the duo's deliberations.

"We have decided on our question, Artichoke," Zed declared.

"Oh, is that so? What's your question, boys?" Artichoke once again took on a human form; this time he looked just like Mr Brow.

"Dad?" Zed cried out.

"No. Just me. I just fancied a change of costume," Artichoke giggled.

Both Hill and Zed thought it was a really cruel and tasteless joke, but they both decided not to comment on it. Artichoke was a little bit disappointed that its humour was missing the mark. It also felt slightly embarrassed that it was so out of practice at interacting with others.

Brushing off the awkward moment, Zed decided to stay on topic and made his request. "Please can you help us find my parents?"

Artichoke smiled. "I knew that's what you would ask me… I will give you an answer in a moment but just to be clear, once I have told you, I cannot speak to you again." Artichoke had a strange way of communicating; Zed and Hill couldn't quite understand why there was a need for all the rules and regulations and, more curiously, why they were shrouded in mystery. The boys both expected a simple, straightforward response, but it was apparent from their verbal exchanges with Artichoke, that was not a likely occurrence.

Artichoke concluded with a final instruction, "Follow the dragonfly."

"Follow the *dragonfly*?" they mouthed to each other with

confusion.

They scoured the room, just in case there was a stray dragonfly flitting about in that small mirrored cube that they hadn't noticed the first time they searched it. Hill and Zed inspected each mirrored wall, nook and cranny, as far as they could stretch their arms to reach, but they came up with nothing.

In a last-ditch attempt, they realised that the only place they hadn't checked was themselves. The boys patted themselves down frantically and, almost immediately, Zed felt something in the right pocket of his checked pyjama trousers. It seemed like a pointy stone, but he was pretty sure that his pockets were empty before he had gone to bed. Zed never stored anything in his nightwear pockets. In fact, he often wondered why there was a need for that feature on night garments. Perhaps to keep a snack, if you woke up in the middle of the night? But then it was likely to get squashed by the weight of a person whilst they slept on it… He thought of it as a very bizarre addition to his pyjamas indeed.

Zed withdrew what looked like a dragonfly shaped rock that had been nestled in his pocket.

"Look!" he called out to Hill. "This must be what Artichoke is talking about!"

Artichoke looked on in amusement, but kept its vow of silence and did not utter a word.

"A stone-carved dragonfly? How on earth is that going to help us?" Hill asked.

Artichoke continued to observe the pair gleefully and then flashed them a knowing smile. They all stared at the dragonfly.

The boys watched in amazement as it twitched ever so slightly.

"Hill! Did you see that? One of the wings flickered. I'm sure of it!" Zed's eyes were fixated on the object in his hand, taking carefully shallow breaths, he did not move any other muscles other than those required for talking.

"Look. There it goes again. Did you see it?" Zed urged. Hill had seen it, but he was in shock. Unable to respond, he gawked on with his mouth agape, anticipating what would happen next.

The stone-dragonfly moved with accelerating vigour and continued to grow with momentum, writhing and shaking until it was able to shed its outer concrete-like shell. Out of the cracked casing emerged a shimmering, golden dragonfly. Once completely free from its cocoon, the dragonfly launched an unsteady takeoff. It appeared as though it was the first time in a long while that it had taken flight, as it flew around erratically, bouncing off all the mirrors around the room and narrowly missing Hill's eyes a few times.

After several minutes of crashing and banging into mirrors, the dragonfly slowly developed confidence and agility as it soared through the room like an elegant, free-spirited ballet dancer. It twirled and whirled around before flying to the top of the cube, steadying itself and then descending determinedly with such great charge; batting its wings with tremendous force, there was only ever going to be one outcome. As it reached the mirrored floor, it created a hole, small and perfectly rounded. This created a ripple effect and caused the ground beneath Hill and Zed to shatter into a million pieces and disappear under them.

Once again, Zed and Hill were swept away unexpectedly, as the mirror beneath them gave way and was sucked into a whirling cyclone. They went crashing through the glass, forced down with a gush of swirling water, as though they were being flushed down a toilet. They descended into the abyss once more.

Welcome To Mirror Maze

They came to the ground with an excruciating bump, further injured by a thick layer of frozen rocks. It was dark and they could just about make out that they were in a cavern, with droplets of water gently tapping on their heads. The air smelled damp and stale.

In the near distance, they could see a clearing. It appeared to be the exit to the cave. The boys stumbled their way through the teeth shaped rocks that scraped across their shins as they fumbled in the gloom.

Soaking wet and desperate for answers, the pair scurried to their feet and frantically searched for the dragonfly who had caused them to plummet to their steep, icy descent.

"Hello!" Zed's voice reverberated out into the uncharted atmosphere. "Is anyone there?"

"I'm here!" Hill called out reassuringly to his friend. "Can you see that dragonfly anywhere?"

"I can hear something… Shh, listen," Zed urged.

Sure enough, in among the vibration of delicate droplets that resounded throughout the cavern, there was the faint but distinct motor-tone of a dragonfly flitting around the cave.

"It's here. I hear it too," Hill confirmed.

Both boys stood perfectly still. Listening, waiting.

The fluttering came to a halt as the dragonfly rested on a rock directly in front of the duo. There was a silence that lasted a few moments. Zed and Hill gazed at the creature with narrowed eyes.

The dragonfly held their gaze. The creature continued to scan them, taking in information as though it were studying not only their faces but the nature of their respective characters.

After an intense exchange, the stand-off concluded when the dragonfly broke the silence with a surprisingly chipper introduction.

"Follow me!" it demanded.

That was its only instruction before gliding through the darkness towards the exit of the cave where it settled on a rock just outside the mouth of the tunnel. The pair scurried after it; they knew they had to keep it in sight. If they allowed it to escape them, so too would their only chance of ever getting back home.

Slowing their sprint to an amble, the duo realised that the dragonfly hadn't been trying to lose them after all, but perhaps rather preferred a change of scenery. Out in the open, the sun was shining, birds were soaring through the warm air and there was a welcomed freshness to the breeze, which was a stark contrast to the dank atmosphere in the sombre cavern.

Hill and Zed soon caught up with the dragonfly, who happily introduced himself. "Hello, I am Dragio, and I am the guide or, should I say, YOUR guide through Mirror Maze Land."

So many questions sprung to mind, but the duo thought it best to take it slow with their inquiries, so they would not make the same mistake they had made when they met Artichoke.

"Hi, Dragio," Hill started tentatively. "Artichoke implied that you would be able to show us where Zed's mum and dad are... Is that true?"

"That's right," Dragio confirmed with a unique chirpiness to his voice. "As I mentioned earlier, I am the guide of Mirror Maze Land, and I have been for an incredibly long while. I know where absolutely everything is – including your parents!"

"Where are they?" Zed hastened to add.

"Ah, all in good time. We'll get there... If you're lucky! Sit down. I've got a few things to share with you before we do." Dragio sank further onto the rock he had perched on and indicated for the duo to join him, with a subtle nod of his head and an outstretched wing.

Dragio had a welcoming aura which the boys picked up on and it allowed them to feel relaxed and at ease even though they were in a strange and unfamiliar land. Perhaps it was his self-assuredness or the fact that he was open to shedding some light on what they were likely to face whilst trying to get back home. Either way, they were glad to have met Dragio as he comforted them simply by being there.

"Time for the *official welcome!*" Dragio announced excitedly. "I'm always keen to get to know different people when they arrive. I guess I shouldn't really but, with every new traveller I meet, I think yes... This could be it."

"It?" the boys both prompted Dragio for further elaboration on that point.

"Yes," Dragio quipped. "You see, Dunkurian is the Empress of Mirror Maze Land and if you're going to succeed, you'll need to know everything about her. It all started like this..."

The Empress

"Millions of moons ago, Dunkurian was banished from her homeland, Esmiatopia, to a barren land for committing crimes against her species, the Kunra. Despite the Kunra's immense stature, calloused, scaly skin and flame-throwing hydrogen glands, this particular breed of flying dragon has a uniquely inherent, kind nature. The Kunra are creatures who are slow to anger but, if pushed, they are formidable enemies. They have the power to devour entire kingdoms, and have done so on more than a few occasions.

"Dunkurian's character is a stark contrast from that of her kin. She is a determined, heartless beast who takes pleasure in inflicting harm on others and, over a sustained period of time, she routinely took advantage of the agreeable disposition of her kin, which upset the balance of nature. The first law of the Kunra is 'Kunra Protects Kunra'. So maintaining this covenant, her clan decided to banish rather than eradicate her.

"The elders who selected her fate authorized Dunkurian to retain some of her powers but ordained that she would never be permitted to return to the realm of Esmiatopia. Faced with eternal exile, an extensive landscape and only her thoughts to occupy her years, Dunkurian's Land became her untainted canvas that she could mould into whatever she desired. Dunkurian proclaimed that her punishment was more of a blessing than a curse. Her altered perception allowed an empty, vast landscape to develop into a safe haven – free from the confines of Kunra Laws. She was The Empress.

"An essential part of her design was to populate her kingdom, and in order to do so, Dunkurian enchanted numerous objects and scattered them throughout various realms. When anyone or anything had the misfortune of engaging with the object, it allowed her to draw them into her realm, the world we now know as Mirror Maze Land.

"The only way to escape the clutches of Dunkurian and this province that she has created is to use her weakness against her. Dunkurian has the power to create her young, but the hatching period lasts two thousand years before an egg reaches maturity. Being of reptilian descent, Dunkruian doesn't need to brood her eggs but she does this as a protective measure. Her eggs are the most important thing to her and she only lays one at a time, so she guards each of them fiercely. The only reason Dunkurian would get off an egg she was in the middle of incubating is to eat, drink or answer the call of nature.

"Dunkurian's goal is to keep her fledgelings safely isolated until they are fit to join Mirror Maze Land in some functional capacity. Her most recent youngling is the lead farmer here, which affords him the privilege of skimming the profits from everything cultivated in Mirror Maze Land.

"After a few months of nurturing with the Empress, the younglings are ready to make it on their own, and they only report back to their mother if events go wrong. Dunkurian hates it when things don't work as planned – informing her of such would mean certain extinction for any being that dared to, even if it happened to be one of her beloved younglings; she is a formidable adversary."

Zed and Hill sat listening to every word that Dragio uttered and gasped at the thought of meeting a creature that took pleasure in harming others. It was a lot for the duo to process and, as scary as it all sounded, they were marginally reassured, because they understood how they all ended up in Mirror Maze Land.

"Ah, so that mirror in my mum and dad's room must have been one of the objects that Dunkurian enchanted!" Zed added, recalling how his mother brought the object back from the recycling centre. "I'm pretty sure the same thing must have happened to the person who owned the mirror before us."

"This is madness," Hill sighed. "So you're telling me there are hundreds – if not thousands… or millions – of these mirrors? This is just…" Hill trailed off as he spun away and tried to catch his breath.

Zed glanced at his friend, took a deep controlled breath and turned to Dragio. "So what about you? Did you find a mirror too?"

Dragio paused for a moment, then sighed nostalgically and smiled. "I want to tell you a story."

A Young Boy

Zed and Hill listened intently, eagerly waiting to hear Dragio's next tale. He was a talented storyteller and Zed admired Dragio's ability to capture and sustain his attention. If only all the teachers who had struggled to teach him over the years could have shared ideas and conveyed information so expertly, he would have enjoyed school a lot more.

***

"A lifetime ago," Dragio began, "there was a young boy who resided on a beautiful, sun-soaked island with his mother and grandmother. His father lived with his other family, but that didn't matter to the youngster. The boy's life was full of appreciation, adventure and, most importantly, love.

"He spent his days at school, where most of his lessons took place outside underneath a mango tree so that all the children could take in the beautiful fresh ocean air. The weather was boiling, so classes were timetabled to finish early in the afternoon, and the boy and his classmates would dance on the beach, with the salty sea air reviving their faces. The cool water was a welcome relief from the unrelenting heat of the sun-baked sand.

"When a crimson glow traversed the sky at each sunset, that was the boy's cue to throw his satchel over his shoulder and head home for his evening meal. Dinner was his favourite time of day.

"His Grandma Bell, or 'Mama-Bell' as he had always called

her, was a talented chef. She owned a local food stand in the municipality centre and crowds would travel for hours to visit her rest stop. People travelled not only for the delectable meals she served up but also for her permanent smile and infectious laughter. Mama-Bell was regarded as a resident hero and the pet name the boy had created for her caught on and all the city folk started calling her that too. She eventually named her shack Mama-Bell's Treats. Her signature dish was a meat stew that she slow-cooked for an age. The meat was so tender, people could remove it from the bone by simply running a spoon through it. There was a special ingredient in Mama-Bell's stew. Instead of using salt, she added sargassum seaweed as a unique flavouring. The only person she let in on her trade secret was her beloved grandson and he knew how important it was for her to have a sustainable supply of the additive.

"The young boy was responsible for collecting the sargassum Mama-Bell used in her cooking. He would do so every Friday afternoon so that she had enough for the hundreds of people that visited her shack each weekend.

"On a Friday, just before the sunset, the boy began his usual routine of diving in the sea to source the priceless sargassum. Once his bucket was full to the brim, he resurfaced and sifted through the seaweed to remove any debris from the container.

"The boy noticed a small seashell, the size of the palm of his hand, that had a mirror on its inner surface. He thought it was odd and wondered what type of creature the husk could have possibly belonged to. As the youngster pondered that notion, he ran his fingers across the shell and then something strange happened. His fingers painlessly scattered into millions of pieces as though his hand had transformed into an infinite number of dry grains of sand. The effect that had started at his fingertips took hold of his arms and then spread to his torso. Before long he could feel himself floating above the water, hovering helplessly above the pail of salty delicacy he had foraged for his beloved Mama-Bell. There was a sharp gust of wind that encircled the fragments of his body and drew them into a ferocious cyclone which spun with such an impressive speed; the boy barely had time to take in what was happening. Within the spiral storm, his particles were rearranged and condensed to create a new being. As the gale behind the boy forced him towards the shell, into the mirror, he caught a glimpse of himself and realised that his body had been remodelled from that of a human child into something else entirely. He was then and forevermore destined to be a dragonfly."

***

"Dragio!" Hill and Zed gasped in complete and utter disbelief.

"You were the little boy!" Zed recoiled in horror. "So that's how you ended up here, in Mirror Maze Land?"

Dragio nodded solemnly. "Yes. Soon after I entered Mirror Maze, Dunkurian found a use for me. She was the one who turned me into a dragonfly and decreed that I spend all eternity here shepherding all who enter Mirror Maze Land."

"That's so sad," Hill said. "It sounds like your Mama-Bell was to you what my mother is to me."

Suddenly the realisation smacked Hill like a kick in the stomach. Dragio was an actual boy, with a real family and legitimate feelings. If it was all ripped away from him in a blink of an eye, then it could certainly happen to Hill. He felt a wave of heat rush across his face and his eyes stung. It took everything he had to fight back the tears from falling. He knew that if he allowed himself to cry then he would be entertaining the idea that he might never see his beloved mother again. It was too much to bear, so he did what he always did. He drew a deep breath in, puffed out his chest and returned the focus to something he had the power to change. Hill refocused his mind on their aim – to find Zed's parents and get out of Mirror Maze Land. Zed, however, was still distracted and intrigued by the life Dragio had lived before being pulled into Mirror Maze Land. He was awed by Dragio's previous existence, which was completely different from anything he had ever experienced. In fact, it was so alien to him it was unfathomable.

Zed had a thousand questions bouncing around his mind, but he began with the most pressing concern. "In all the time you've spent here, you've never found a way out?"

"Well…" Dragio sighed. "There is definitely a way out; there always is… The only problem is you have to have the right skills and resources."

That hopeful response from Dragio was exactly what Hill needed to hear. Not all was lost. Hill perked up, before adding, "Will you help us find the way out?"

"We could help each other!" Zed squealed. "You could finally be reunited with your family!"

"I don't know if my world still exists," Dragio replied solemnly, with a sigh.

Riding the wave of positivity, Hill quipped, "If Dunkurian had the power to create an entire empire by siphoning resources from other realms – as she did by drawing us all in here – then I'm pretty sure if anyone has the ability to send you back to your world it would be her. You said that all we needed were the right 'skills and resources', true?" Dragio offered Hill a considered nod in response. "Well, I think that between the three of us, we would make an excellent team."

At that moment the duo became a trio, and they vowed to look out for each other and protect one another in their fight towards their shared goal, to get themselves and Zed's parents out of Mirror Maze Land.

Dragio revealed that it was essential that they collected a "sample" from the Lake of Life first, which was one of the earliest features of Mirror Maze Land. He disclosed that each Kunra, including Dunkurian, has an ever-burning, water-resistant flame at the end of their tail. Their tails are the source of their magic and, without that, they are temporarily vulnerable to attack. Dragio stressed that the effect of their extinguished flames would not last very long, so they would have to work quickly.

Whilst cultivating Mirror Maze Land, Empress Dunkurian wanted to ensure that if the elders were to one day develop a change of heart and decide to harm her, she would have quick access to the Lake of Life so that she could render them powerless and attack them first before they regenerated their flames.

One aspect Dragio withheld from the story was rather significant. The thing that made the water so special, was the fact that it was home to a rare, bright yellow species of leech, native to her homeland. A secretion from their skin mixed with the water particles gives it an extraordinary property. The unique liquid is the only substance that can extinguish the otherwise never-ending Kunra fire.

The Lake Of Life

The trio didn't have far to travel to the lake as it was close to the cave they had cascaded into after leaving Artichoke in the glass cube. An insect-eating plant grew close to the water's edge which quite conveniently, doubled up as a vessel to carry a sample of liquid. The plant had a lid that could open to entice insects in and then snap shut the moment it trapped one. Dragio pointed out the plant to the pair and Hill plucked one from its bed.

As they stood at the shore at the glistening water's edge, it all looked so clear and inviting. The Lake of Life was still. It had a distinct, beautifully sweet scent that wafted over the water.

"What is that beautiful smell?" Hill asked, taking a deep breath in.

"It's not as *sweet* as you think…" Dragio started, but before he had a chance to finish his explanation, Hill jumped into the deceptively clear lake, swam into the middle and stood up triumphantly, with the plant, full of the substance needed to extinguish Kunra flames. Zed and Dragio looked at each other and burst into fits of laughter.

"What?" Hill asked. "You should come in and join me," he called out. "This water is amazing. It's warm and luxurious, like one of my mum's seaweed bubble baths!"

"That's definitely not seaweed!" Zed blurted, barely able to contain his amusement.

"Yes… um… you've got… got a little something on your eyebrow there, Hill," Dragio explained as he continued to cackle.

Hill reached up to touch his left eyebrow and nestled neatly on the top of it, was a gelatinous mass. He tried to wipe it off, but it didn't budge.

"Um... I was just about to tell you... the lake is full of leeches!" Dragio called out and the realisation hit.

Hill screamed high-pitched yelps whilst wading his way out of the gloopy mixture. He was reluctant to put his head under the surface again for fear of getting one in his mouth.

As he stepped out of the water, he noticed that his body was covered in fluorescent yellow leeches. Hill had never seen one up close before, never mind have them dotted all over his expansive frame. He cried out for help, but Zed had fallen to the ground. The force of his laughter caused his legs to give up their primary function as he struggled to catch his breath.

"I'm sorry... I'm sorry... it's just... too... funny." That was pretty much the only sentence that he could string together.

Hill, mildly annoyed and extremely terrified, dropped to the floor and started squashing the leeches attached to his body by rolling around in the dirt. This seemed to do the trick.

Before long, he was free from the creatures but covered in red blotches all over his skin.

After finally regaining his composure, Zed couldn't help but tease his friend one more time. "I am sorry, Hill. I'm just glad it wasn't me. I was so tempted to jump in too and almost did until I noticed your face! Those things looked disgusting."

"Thanks," Hill retorted with playful sarcasm. He also saw the funny side once he was free from infestation. The encounter had reminded him of when he went on holiday with his mum and got stung by a jellyfish "That was much worse," he recounted. "At least the leeches didn't hurt."

"You've been on holiday?" Zed asked.

"Yes. We go every year. It's just the best —" Hill stopped

himself from describing how amazing holidays were when he saw the deflation in Zed's eyes.

"I have never been on holiday with my parents," Zed disclosed with a sigh. "I would be happy if they had some interest in me and maybe took me to the park or to a museum once in a while. They are so busy with their own lives, they don't take much notice of me."

Zed wasn't upset about the fact that Hill had been on holiday or (arguably) had the best mother in the world. His meagre existence saddened him when he compared the stories that Dragio and Hill had both shared with him, to his limited life experiences.

Zed loved his parents greatly but had always secretly wished that they had adopted him. He created cartoon sketches in his art book back at home in the flat of his original parents and even wrote biography profiles for them. Zed imagined that his first mum and dad were fabulously rich billionaires that adored him, but they felt they needed to give him up for adoption because their lives were too demanding as a jet-setting business couple, travelling the world. His real folks would have appreciated him in their hearts, but they were too busy hopping from one boardroom to the next to nurture an infant successfully. Zed also imagined that his parents were incredibly generous, and another factor in their decision-making was that they took pity on a poor, unfortunate couple (Mr and Mrs Brow) who were unable for whatever reason to have a baby of their own.

Zed had even named his imaginary biological parents. In the corporate field, everyone knew them as Angelica Stone and Bertram Stone. They were a formidable couple in business, but he affectionately referred to them as Mama and Papa Stone, in his mind.

Dragio jolted Zed back to reality with a query. "If your parents don't notice you and don't spend time with you, then why are you so keen to find them and take them back to your world?"

"That's a good question!" Hill agreed.

"I know I am not the luckiest boy in the world..." Zed started, nodding at Hill, implying that perhaps Hill was the luckiest. "...But my parents are mine I guess, and for better or worse, they are all that I have."

Both Hill and Dragio nodded in acknowledgement. They understood why Zed's parents were important to him, even if they weren't perfect!

Jibber Jabber Forest

After an arduous journey along a humid and dusty road, the trio reached what Dragio referred to as Jibber Jabber Forest.

"What's *that*?" the boys cried out.

"Well… Nothing is as it seems… This is the point in Mirror Maze Land where most people fail by falling victim to Dunkurian's enchanted landscape. They lose their sense of reality and forgo the opportunity to leave forever. Dunkurian then finds a use for them as a permanent resident of Mirror Maze Land."

"Isn't there another way to get to Dunkurian?" Zed quizzed, "You know this place better than anyone. Can we take another route around Jibber Jabber Forest?"

"I wish there was, but this is the only path," Dragio assured them. "I'm rooting for you and will be with you, guiding your every step. We have to do this!" Dragio urged Zed. "The best strategy you can use is to walk briskly; look straight ahead – not down – and NEVER look up!"

Dragio's introduction to Jibber Jabber Forest was frightening, mostly because it was such a stern warning but also because Zed and Hill didn't quite understand what they were being warned against. Dragio stressed how important it was for them to follow his instructions, and he relayed the plan to them for a second time. "I will fly within your sightlines and hum one of my favourite songs – one that my Mama-Bell used to sing to me when I was scared. It helped me to be brave and it'll help you to stay focused on me and not on anything that might… or rather, *will* happen around you. If we are going to get through this, we need to stick to the plan – stay together!"

Zed and Hill gawked at each other, each willing the other to offer some additional form of reassurance. They shuffled towards each other.

"It's now or never," Zed affirmed with a clasp of Hill's hand.

"Now or never!" Hill echoed. "Let's do this!"

Zed's palm slid away from Hill's grasp. Feeling slightly embarrassed, he wiped his palms across his chest and drew a sharp exhale before reclaiming a drier grip. Not wishing to highlight the attention to Zed's anxiety, Hill simply offered his friend a knowing smile.

***

Initially, the forest looked like any other: a sea of various shades of green droplets against a canvas of brown. Once they were fully surrounded by the woodland trees, the branches extended their reach towards the trio as though seeking comfort.

Zed and Hill picked up the pace from a steady march to a jog in a bid to get through the experience as quickly as possible. Their collective gaze was firmly focused on Dragio, who flew swiftly and steadily at eye level as promised, and called out occasionally to prevent Hill and Zed from getting distracted by their surroundings.

The leaves around them whispered inaudible messages, and the sound increased in volume and intensity the more they tried to ignore the mumbling. They picked up the pace to a sprint and the voices grew louder and louder until one vocalisation stood out from the rest and became crystal clear. That voice was warm and incredibly familiar to both Hill and Zed.

"Franky?... It's me, your mother. I'm here! Where are you?"

Hill stopped dead in his tracks. He would recognise that tone anywhere. It was his mum! Was she really in Mirror Maze Land too?

Perhaps she woke up in the night and realised that he was not in the comfort of his bed and then took the logical step of following him to Zed's flat. He had to find her.

"It's my mum!" he called out to Dragio and Zed, also causing them to halt and look back.

"It is not your mother!" Dragio warned him impatiently. "That's what Jibber Jabber Forest wants you to think… Keep moving. Don't stop!"

The warning came too late for Hill. He had already looked up through the trees above him and was immediately mesmerized by what he saw.

The foliage above them parted and behind a curtain of green, there were dazzling lights dancing their way across the sky. Shocking oranges, greens, reds, blues and purple smoke plumes bounced across the sky. Hill was stunned, and he could not move, other than to breathe shallow breaths of air, in and out of his expansive chest.

Zed and Dragio called out to Hill, but he could not hear them. Moving for the first time in several moments, Hill stretched his arms out above his head, calling out to the trees. One tree in particular responded to his summons as it lifted him off the ground with a branch that encircled his chest.

"No," Zed screamed as he reached for his companion.

The tree elevated Hill at such an impressive speed and all Zed could hold on to was Hill's foot. He pulled with every ounce of energy he had. He would not lose his best friend. Not today, not ever!

Zed's face was red with determination as he clung on with

his might. Every ounce of strength he owned in every fibre of his being. Then he let out an almighty growl.

The shock of Zed's grisly tone snapped Hill out of his trance and Hill fought for his life. He pulled the branch towards his mouth and bit down as hard as he could. The tree groaned in pain and loosened its grip on Hill which allowed him to wriggle free from its grasp.

As Hill came crashing down to the dirt, Dragio breathed a temporary sigh of relief — he warned them that they were not out of Jibber Jabber Forest yet and instructed them to keep moving. The boys leapt to their feet and ran — knowing that their lives depended on it.

They sprinted for what felt like an age until they finally came to a clearing in the woodland. The rays of light reflected through the trees temporarily stifled their delicate eyesight.

"I've never run so much in my entire life... Please don't make me do that ever again!" Hill panted as they all drew a moment to collapse into a heap, with Dragio draped across Zed's hairline.

The trio took the time to appreciate that they were nevertheless still alive, daring to breathe an extended sigh of relief and a well-earned embrace.

The Mercreature

Before long, they set off to continue their journey towards Dunkurian's palace. Dragio informed Hill and Zed that they were approaching Soggy Bog, which he warned would be more challenging than Jibber Jabber Forest. He also stressed that only a handful of people had successfully navigated their way through to the other side of Soggy Bog.

Hill winced and Zed plastered a smile across his face. His smile would have been convincing had it not been for the stark fear in his eyes. Dragio sensed the anxiety within the group and, even though he knew that being the Mirror Maze Land guide meant that he would be protected in all eventualities, he felt the pressure for them to succeed. Not because Hill and Zed were his ticket out of Mirror Maze Land, but because he had grown attached to the courteous and caring duo and considered them as friends.

Trudging through the barren landscape, tiredness and fatigue set in for all of them, but none of them wanted to be the first to express it outwardly. After some internal deliberation, Hill had no choice but to point out how exhausted he was after he tripped on a twig and tumbled to the ground. He found it impossible to get up once he was down on the floor.

"It's rather comfy down here I have to admit." Hill smirked, trying to mask his embarrassment.

"I guess we could all do with a little sit-down," Zed agreed with a sigh of relief.

Dragio echoed Zed's sigh as he looked out into the horizon.

Perplexed, Hill gazed up at Dragio, who had settled on Zed's shoulder, "I didn't realise that dragonflies got tired of flying," he quipped.

"Everyone gets tired, eventually," Dragio rebuffed. "Although it's not that," he added.

"What's wrong?" Zed asked.

"Now and then I get flashbacks to the time when I lived at home, my real home I mean. I just remembered... Sow-Sow." Zed and Hill could almost see him salivating.

"Sow-Sow?" Hill queried.

Dragio explained that it was a unique plant that only grew underneath the water of the Great Lake. Once plucked from the seabed, it should be pickled in a unique marinade for months before it reaches the optimum flavour. Dragio described waiting for what felt like a lifetime between each batch that his mother had prepared. The finished product was a spicy, pickled vegetable, which was really only reserved for special occasions. Most people only ate it once a year but, in his household, they would always eat it four or five times a year because his mother knew how much he loved it!

It was incredibly risky, sourcing the raw plant, because typically it was a merperson delicacy. It was a fiercely guarded resource and if a mercreature found anything other than their own kind pilfering the Sow-Sow, they would turn it into a small fish. If a fish, however, dared to nibble the protected plant, then it would be banished from the Great Lake and cast into a miniature muddy pond.

The story was incredibly intriguing to both Hill and Zed. They had never heard anything like it. Hill had read an awful lot of books in his spare time and although he had come across the legend of merpeople, he never truly believed they existed.

Dragio shared how he had a close encounter with a mercreature. Funnily enough, it was not on one of the many occasions where he had been foraging for Sow-Sow.

***

One Summer morning, Dragio awoke earlier than everyone else in the house. The sun peeped into his bedroom through the mosquito-mesh covered windows and the cockerels welcomed the dawn.

Drenched in sweat from the humidity of the night before, Dragio decided to take a trip to the river to freshen up. He would often go there in the mornings, particularly in the height of summer. Most people stayed in bed a little later and he had the water all to himself. That morning did not differ from any other, or so he thought.

Having thrown his bathing towel over his shoulder, Dragio sprinted down to the lake which was a relatively short journey. He loved singing and it would usually take him about the time required to sing a verse and a chorus of one of his favourite traditional hymns. His grandmother always sang when she was cooking and somehow, without being explicitly taught, Dragio could recite each chorus, verse, bridge and ad-lib perfectly. He often sang without realising, almost on auto-pilot. It was definitely a trait that ran in the family.

The lake was calm as usual. A glowing orange sunrise nestled at eye-line in the distance painted the vast horizon. The shoreline was littered with enormous boulders, which were useful for sitting on whilst dipping your toes in the water. They were also convenient storage devices for articles of clothing whilst taking a dip.

Dragio took off his slippers and rolled up his towel around them, creating a ball, and then lackadaisically perching the items on the edge of the largest rock he could find.

He winced as he dipped a leg in. That first step always caused a shock to his system but Dragio knew that the quicker he submerged his full body, the sooner he would feel the lake's calming effect that would rejuvenate him. He dropped backwards and allowed his weight to be carried. Dragio strayed out further, deeper into the pool, as he gently lapped the still water beneath his palms. He loved being outdoors and close to nature. Although a sociable child, he truly valued the beauty of spending time alone, in the lake.

As he lay back, barely moving a muscle, Dragio felt a large scaly fin brush past his leg. He imagined that it was a tropical fish; the reservoir wasn't short of marine life. He would regularly come into contact with creatures he had never seen before. Dragio had conditioned himself to expect the unexpected. That was just a typical day at the lake.

Dragio glanced over his shoulder and glimpsed a shimmering tail. Driven by his curiosity, Dragio peered underneath the water. What he saw was unlike anything he could have ever imagined. Frozen with shock, he studied the creature intently and his intrigue was equally reciprocated.

The creature's upper body resembled that of a fully formed human male; the lower half was similar to that of a gigantic snapper fish. The length of its tail alone was longer than Dragio's entire body. Its scales were splashed with dazzling colours that shimmered from one shade to the next every time it inhaled. The creature had its mouth open and as Dragio peered inside. He noticed that within its human-shaped mouth there were countless rows of miniature fish teeth.

In the distance, there was a faint sound of a horn. It was a calling of some sort – one that Dragio had never heard before. Locked in their gaze of mutual fascination, the creature of the lake broke eye contact, shrieked at him exposing its elongated serrated tongue before swimming off so quickly that Dragio questioned whether the encounter had actually happened. Whether he had really come face to face with a mercreature!

***

"What?" Zed and Hill recoiled in disbelief at Dragio's recount.

"I don't believe you!" Zed quipped. "So why didn't it turn you into a small fish then?" he pressed.

Dragio rolled his eyes. "They only do that if they catch you eating their Sow-Sow. You don't have to accept that what I am saying is factual." Dragio continued, "Actually I'd probably think you were lying if you told me that story, but it's true. It really did happen!"

Zed sniggered quietly to himself, still unconvinced that the event ever occurred.

Soggy Bog

There was a foul stench of rotting sewage with a hint of faeces that wafted through the air. Extremely sensitive to aromas, Zed was the first one to scrunch his face and grab his nose.

"What is that awful whiff?" he demanded.

Hill, slightly slower on the uptake, breathed in deeply before he felt the full force of the assault on his nasal cavities. "Yuk!" he yelled, doubling over in horror and fruitlessly trying to waft away the air in front of him.

"That, my friends…" Dragio began, looking rather smug as he had grown accustomed to the stench and no longer experienced the same degree of discomfort as Hill and Zed did. "That is Soggy Bog!"

"Well, it definitely has the stink associated with a bog. It smells like boiled eggs and rotten fish heads. It's disgusting!" Hill concluded.

Dragio found their dramatic reactions hilarious. He reminisced back to the time when he had first encountered Soggy Bog. He realised that he most definitely responded in a similar way. "Don't worry, you'll soon grow used to the smell," Dragio explained.

"I would really rather not get used to it," Hill joked, beginning to see the amusing side of things.

"On a serious note," Dragio warned them, "we have to stay focused for this next part. You need to watch every single step that you take because the mud has a habit of opening up and swallowing people – whole!"

Zed and Hill gasped. Zed wondered if it was just one of Dragio's elaborate stories or if indeed it was a possibility that he would become a delectable meal for the bog.

Dragio flew up incredibly high and then called down to Hill and Zed. "Hey, you two. Come and join me!"

Hill picked up on what Dragio had alluded to and immediately began to scale a rock that resembled the side of a mountain.

"How do you expect me to get up there?" Zed queried from below.

"Climb up!" Hill retorted unhelpfully. He was surprisingly agile for his size.

"You're fast!" Dragio pointed out.

"Thanks. Cubs!"

Dragio appeared confused. "Cubs? What's that?"

"It's a survival club I go to once a week. They've taught me a whole heap of useful skills. I know a lot about plants and all the extraordinary things we can use them for. Once, my mum had an awful cold. She could barely get out of bed in the morning. I boiled lots of roots together, like they showed us at survival camp, and guess what? She was fine by teatime!"

Hill looked down from the top of the rock he was perched on, whilst Zed was still clasping on at the base. Dragio and Hill stared at each other, shook their heads and chuckled between themselves.

"So, that is Soggy Bog?" Hill asked, gazing out at the misty landscape.

"This is what I wanted you to see," Dragio affirmed. "It looks like a relatively short distance to get across Soggy Bog, but the main challenge is trying to make it from one end to the next without getting swallowed by the gurgling muddy puddles… See that there?... Look!"

Hill and Dragio looked on as a petite, blue chested bird hovered above a puddle.

"Watch carefully," Dragio urged Hill.

The bird spotted a little berry that had fallen from a nearby tree. Its wings stopped fluttering temporarily as it settled onto the ground. Not indeed a moment later the bird was sucked into the muddy puddle without any warning.

Hill gasped.

"What? What is it?" Zed called from the base of the rock. He still hadn't managed to scale it. He had given up clinging to the base and accepted that, even with all the best will in the world, there was no way that he could possibly make it to the top.

Hill looked down at Zed with furrowed eyebrows and yelled, "You'd better learn to climb pretty quickly if we're going to make it through there alive!"

Hill formulated a plan. The idea was to lay sticks on the floor, so they could use them to stand on, but as soon as they put a branch down it got swallowed up by the gurgling ground beneath it. They tried to implement the strategy a few times, but they kept achieving the same result. With each stick that the Bog gulped, a loud burp succeeded.

Dragio suggested that they climb a tree and swing through the branches. "Easy for you to say!" Zed retorted. "We are not kids from a jungle movie!"

Hill found that hilarious as he scaled the first tree.

Zed corrected his statement, whilst staring up in awe. "Okay, maybe *some* of us are not characters from a film."

After an effortful shuffle up the first tree, Zed developed his own unique way of soaring. He hugged the wood tightly with his entire body and shifted one limb at a time, centimetre by centimetre. His strategy closely resembled that of a sloth hanging from the tree trunk, but he didn't care. Not one bit. He was climbing, and that was worthy of a celebration... If only he could raise a triumphant fist, he would, but he could barely raise a smile. Dragio acknowledged the struggle Zed was facing by bursting into spontaneous song. It was an old one, but a pleasant one. The lyrics conjured images of successfully conquering heights, and of brave warriors finally achieving their goals. Dragio remembered it because it was the song that his mother sang for him on his first day of school, the first night he slept in his own bed and all the other times when he needed to dig a little deeper to find his inner courage.

Feeling inspired, Zed's eyes narrowed. He was determined to conquer the tree he clung to, and each subsequent one that stood in the way of him and his freedom. He was on a roll. Zed felt like a leopard, hesitantly hopping from branch to branch.

Just past the halfway point through Soggy Bog, Zed balanced the entirety of his weight on what he thought was a tree trunk, but he missed his step and snapped the pencil-thin twig beneath it.

Zed fell head first towards the bubbling mud stew. His left foot got wedged between two branches, which left him dangling upside down, rigid with fright.

The snap of the twig had caught Hill's attention, and he gasped in horror, being mindful not to panic Zed further for fear that he would go plummeting to his death. Dragio continued humming his tune, desperately trying to muffle his anxiety. The song had become a coping device, more for his own benefit rather than Zed's at that point.

Hill, who was already three trees ahead, retreated backwards, straddled the tree Zed was dangling from and reached for his arm, which was just out of range. "Give me your hand!" he demanded.

Zed tried to achieve a sit-up mid-air but was he unsuccessful on each attempt. In fact, he felt his foot loosen ever so slightly with each thrust upwards.

"It's no use. I can feel myself slipping down. Help me. Please!" he screamed.

He peered down at the ground beneath him and quivered as Soggy Bog began aiming shots of steaming mud at Zed as though it were salivating at the thought of swallowing him whole.

At that moment, Hill had a flashback to one of his weekend retreats with his scouts club, and his survival training kicked in. He snapped two twigs from the branch above his head and rubbed them together with a furious intensity.

"What are you doing?" Zed called up to his friend.

With Hill just out of his sight-line, all he could hear was the sound associated with friction. What worried him most was the vibrations emanating from the timber that barely had a grip of his foot, and he felt himself slip down even further.

"What are you doing, Hill?" Dragio echoed as he noticed the detrimental effect of the shaking tree.

"Camp!" That is all that Hill could muster in response, sweating profusely from the prolonged effort, focused on the sticks. Dragio and Zed had no idea what he was talking about.

A spark flickered briefly before a thin veil of smoke followed. Hill blew with a steady stream of air between the two tiny sticks… There was another ignition, a flame and the unmistakable smell of charring. Yes! He had done it.

Hill grinned as the fire grew, nurturing the smoke between his hands. When he deemed the fire as established, he threw the burning twigs on to the ground.

With the flames swelling beneath him, Zed became uncomfortably warm. He was convinced that if Soggy Bog didn't eat him alive, then he would surely fall into the expanding fire beneath him.

Dragio also panicked as he tried to redirect the flares away from Zed's head by flapping his wings furiously at the fire. The only issue was, his 'help' had an adverse effect. The burning twigs were engulfed by the flames. Hill also began to doubt himself and wondered whether he had made a colossal mistake, as he watched from above.

Moments later, the muddy soup opened up and swallowed the fire underground. They all stared in disbelief, at the spot where the fire had been. The gloop had dried up, hardened and cracked beneath Zed.

Taking full advantage of the welcomed opportunity, Hill sprung into action. He leapt down from the tree like a graceful gazelle onto the parched ground and tugged at Zed's trapped foot.

Within seconds, Hill released his friend, who crashed to the floor with a thud. But Zed didn't feel an ounce of pain, only an overwhelming sense of relief that he was finally free from the tree's grasp.

Dragio didn't spare a moment for respite. He urged both Hill and Zed to get back into the tree as quickly as possible. He had never seen anyone perform a trick on Soggy Bog like that before and, being in the uncharted territory, he was not completely sure how long the dehydrated patch would stay moistureless for. Taking heed of Dragio's warning, the pair swiftly scaled the tree. Even Zed was notably faster at clambering up the tree compared to his earlier attempts. He would not waste his second chance.

Zed scaled a third of the way up the timber, and then there was a ground-shifting quake which almost knocked them both off the tree again. The violent tremor was followed by a gurgle and then a burp louder than they could have ever imagined. It was so loud that they all temporarily lost their hearing. After extinguishing the fire, Soggy Bog spat out the sticks and sent them soaring into the air, so high in fact that they reached the clouds, before crashing back down into the gloopy gunge with a plop!

Hill, Zed and Dragio stood still to compose themselves, struggling to process all that had happened in the last few moments. After catching their breaths for a moment they managed to navigate their path out of Soggy Bog by leaping from branch to branch, ensuring to avoid all twigs on the way out.

The Palace

Standing at the apex of a ravine, just north of Soggy Bog, Dragio pointed out what looked like a tiny house in the centre of the horizon, surrounded by a moat.

"We're here," he announced triumphantly. "That over there is the heartbeat of Mirror Maze Land. That is where Dunkurian resides," he added with an air of apprehension.

The trio exchanged glances before refocusing their attention ahead. Zed mustered the courage to admit that, despite being armed with a sample of liquid from the Lake of Life, all they had was a skeleton of a plan at best.

"Don't worry, we've got this!" Hill chirped, waving the cupped flower containing essence from the lake of life.

"Careful with that!" Dragio shrieked at him.

"All right, okay," Hill snapped back as he sheepishly pocketed the plant.

In a bid to flesh out their strategy, Zed asked, "Where are my parents exactly? Are they in there?" Nodding towards the palace in the distance.

Dragio offered a dry laugh.

"Your mother…" he began, "Told Dunkurian that she wanted to be rich, so rich in fact that she would have more than she could ever spend in a lifetime."

Zed rolled his eyes as he mumbled, "Treasures… Yes, that sounds like my mum."

"Indeed. She was quite insistent and Dunkurian was happy to oblige."

"Huh? Really? From what I've heard so far about Dunkurian, I find that hard to believe."

"Well believe it. She locked your mother in the basement of the palace, surrounded by gold, gems, jewels and notes from every currency she could think of. She also has some of the finest clothing you could ever imagine and over fourteen thousand pairs of shoes. I understand she has counted them all. Of course, that's all she'll be doing with them."

Zed's face dropped. He understood that his mother's dream was being used as a means of torture for her.

"Where's Dad? Is he with her?"

"They had totally different desires. He longed for a life outdoors."

"My dad? Really? He's usually at work or sleeping!"

"Exactly," Dragio confirmed. "Funny how we always want what we don't have isn't it?"

"Ah!" Zed got it. He felt the same. When he was at school, he yearned to be elsewhere; at home, he regularly escaped into his imaginary art world; and when his parents disappeared, he wanted more than anything to be with them.

***

On the approach to the palace, Zed and Hill were taken aback by its grandeur. They'd never seen anything like it. Up close, its facade was so immense, it was impossible to see where the sides curved to create a unique dome shape.

Intricate carvings of animals were engraved into the marble wall, which had been delicately painted with gold leaf. The ornate external features signified that it was a palatial abode, fit for an empress.

It was surprisingly quiet outside the palace. There was a faint bleating of some nearby mountain goats and the distinct clucking of some seemingly excited hens.

"That'll be him." Dragio indicated with a fixed stare.

Hill and Zed glanced behind their shoulders.

"Dad! Dad!" Zed cried out as he turned and ran towards the figure of a pale, sickly-looking man dishing out grains to a flock of frantic chickens.

"Zeddie-bear!" Mr Brow hollered back affectionately. He hadn't called him that in over five years. Zed couldn't quite recall the precise moment or reason that affectionate term of endearment was retired from use, but he warmly welcomed it. Zed stopped short, just in front of his father. He was barely recognisable; it felt like a lifetime since he'd last seen him.

A hug was a stretch too far for Mr Brow to offer so, instead, he extended an arm and tenderly ruffled Zed's – now matted – curly mop. That was enough for him. It was the most physical contact he could have hoped for from his dad, and certainly the most he'd received in his living memory.

Hill approached with caution as father and son continued their peculiar interaction.

Suddenly realisation hit and Mr Brow's smile morphed into woe as he admired his child and stroked his cheek. "My poor boy. I'm so sorry."

"Don't worry, Dad, we've got a plan!" Zed said optimistically. "We found you, didn't we?"

"Yes, son. I suppose you did."

Zed introduced his father to Hill, who was pleased that he could finally put a face to the name. Hill thought he looked like a weathered version of Zed. Mr Brow quickly warmed to Hill; he was so grateful that Zed had met someone who had been able to look out for him.

The next phase of the plan was to locate Mrs Brow, before confronting Dunkurian. So they set off towards the palace entrance together. As they stood by the doors of the palace, they felt the walls reverberating with a low-pitched growl. Dragio explained that it was a comforting sound because it meant that Dunkurian was asleep. If there's one thing she valued more than her hatchlings, it was her rest. During her daily slumber, she demanded that everyone within the dwelling disappeared elsewhere or, failing that, they would have to tiptoe and whisper so as not to interrupt her. No soul dared to risk the wrath of the exhausted beast.

It did not come as a surprise that the palace basement, which imprisoned Mrs Brow, was unguarded. She lay with her back towards the cage's gate, casually throwing coins at the wall in front of her. She had used a jewel's structural integrity to her advantage and carved out an image of a large scaly beast that resembled Dunkurian. Mrs Brow cheered hysterically every time she struck a section of the creature.

From a distance, she was unrecognisable to Zed and Mr Brow. She appeared delirious and oblivious to the impending tiptoeing of her liberators.

"Mum?" Zed managed to restrict his tone to a mandatory whisper. His mother, however, took no notice of the supposed ban on raised voices. She continued to yelp with delight after every coin toss.

"Is she always like this?" Hill asked, unsure of whether he ought to be pleased or concerned.

"She's been isolated for a while now," Dragio explained with a shrug. "No creature dares to venture down here for fun. It happens to them all, eventually."

Zed, now close enough to touch her, reached an arm through the metal bars and stroked her matted locks. Mrs Brow did not acknowledge her son's presence but instead hummed a comforting tune to herself, whilst stroking a gold bar which she cradled like a baby.

"We have to get her out of there!" Zed's words were stifled as he swallowed hard in a bid to battle the tears that singed from within. "Mummy? Look at me, please, Mum." He urged her further, but she did not respond to him.

"Look, over there, behind that painting on the wall." Dragio directed the group. "You will find a little leaver. Push it up and that will disengage the lock. Hurry, though. We do not want to get caught down here."

Leaping into action, Zed shot across the floor, located the switch and pushed it up. The gate slowly crept open, but its rusty bars scraped across each other and made a terrible racket.

Mrs Brow halted her melodious humming and turned to look at the figures that stood behind her.

"Hello," she grinned cordially whilst bowing her head in an attempt at a curtsey as she extended an arm out to Mr Brow, who was in complete shock. "How do you do?"

"Mum. It's us!" Zed smiled, hoping for a spark of recognition.

"Lovely to meet you too, little man."

"Let's not waste time," Hill urged the group. "Let's just get to Durkurian's egg, before she finds us!"

There was no protest as they all nodded in agreement and turned to exit the basement via the stairs they descended. Mr Brow took Mrs Brow's arm and shuffled towards the door with a skipped-step marking the urgency.

"Wait!" Dragio shouted. No longer taking notice of the

whisper rule.

"What is it?" Zed panicked.

"Do you hear that?"

"No!" They all shook their heads in response.

"Exactly!"

Zed and Hill gasped as the realisation sank in. "She's... AWAKE!"

Mrs Brow was still oblivious to the commotion, and she grinned whilst swaying rhythmically to music, which was inaudible to the ears of others, and then burst into song.

"Shh, please stop that, dear!" Mr Brow urged, but she didn't pay any attention to him. If anything, she was further inspired to float around the room.

Between them, the group tried to hush Mrs Brow by ping-ponging between pleading with her, demanding her silence, comforting her and desperately trying to convey the importance of her compliance.

Nothing worked.

They all ushered her towards the top of the stairs, dragged an oblivious Mrs Brow up to the last step and Hill reached for the exit handle. He carefully drew the door back towards him and peered out of it.

The corridor was empty and silent. Exhaling with relief, Hill signalled to the others that the coast was clear. One by one, they shuffled out of the basement into the long passageway that continued for an age.

The hallway was dimly lit with candles strategically placed on either side of the walkway to ensure staff could manoeuvre from one end of the windowless corridor to the next.

Dragio's knowledge of the underbelly of the mansion allowed them to stealthily navigate their way in and out of unused rooms and unfrequented corridors until they finally reached the main hall – the heart of the palace. The entrance was a double-door, made from solid gold, adorned with gemstones around its frame. Two crystal door handles sat in the centre.

There was no going back. Dragio led the pack. Being the smallest, he was able to enter through a crack in the door fairly easily without being spotted by anyone.

The room was a genuine reflection of Dunkurian's opulent taste. It was adorned with grandiose chandeliers, the finest silk curtains and solid gold and platinum chairs. The reception hall was the place where Dunkurian spent most of her time whilst at home, so it was the most magnificent room of them all.

Dragio signalled to the others that the coast was clear. The group tiptoed and shuffled into the hall where, at first glance, they located a huge, plush cushion the size of a bus, situated in the centre of the chamber on the floor. Nestled in its centre was exactly what they were looking for: Dunkurian's unguarded egg, and an opportunity to grab it!

As they scurried closer towards the highly sought after egg, the vast double-doors they had entered through slammed shut.

The Meeting

The group feared that their nightmare had become a reality. They stopped dead in their tracks and froze at the very moment the door slammed shut. Mrs Brow, who was still unaware of what was unfolding, continued with her meandering towards the double windows to admire the palace gardens.

"What are you doing here?" Dunkurian bellowed with a profound bass that caused an almighty quake within the dwelling walls and unsteadied the group's collective stance. "How dare you break into my sanctuary!"

Fraught with anxiety, Dragio scrambled to explain why they were there without causing suspicion. "Um... Empress... er... we... er, we, we, just came for a visit as part of the deluxe tour." Dragio smiled humbly, in a desperate attempt to mask his deception.

She scowled. "There is no such thing. You know very well that my chambers are strictly out of bounds for everyone except *me*!"

Mrs Brow pranced towards Dunkurian, dazzling her with spins and gyrations, while the rest of her party gazed on in disbelief. Snapping into action with his swift thinking, Zed seized the opportunity to grasp the unguarded egg, while Dunkurian was momentarily perplexed by his mother's, unintentional, perfectly timed distraction.

A brief moment later, Dunkurian realised that Zed was heading for her precious egg.

"NO!" She thundered, shooting a nasal flare towards Zed,

which barely missed his bottom.

As he dodged the range of the flame, Zed unwittingly ventured further away from the prize than he had hoped. Cornered, with his back up against the window, Zed locked eyes with the formidable beast.

Hill and Mr Brow rushed towards Dunkurian, with the aim of straddling her shoulders in a bid to restrain her. Their plan was thwarted when Dunkurian brushed them aside, as though they were insignificant nuisances, with a single sweep of her tail which knocked them both out cold.

Dragio was left stunned, unable to help in any way other than to plead with the angry beast who, in her state of fury, refused to even acknowledge Dragio's presence.

Dunkurian inched closer to Zed, so close that her smouldering breath suffocated him. Locked in a steely stare, he had nowhere to go, so he stood there, frozen.

"You dare to rest your gaze on one of my eggs? WHY?" she demanded, spitting streams of fire, as she crept nearer to him. The base in Dunkurian's roar was deafening. She prowled towards Zed and clasped his leg between her teeth. She flapped her immense wings and prepared to take flight, while Zed hung upside down from her mouth and screamed for someone to help him.

The flapping caused a whirlwind within the palace, which brought Hill back to consciousness. He leapt up from the floor and hurled the closed cup flower containing water from the Lake of Life towards Dunkurian's flaming tail. He missed completely and the liquid splashed all over the silk curtains that draped over the windows instead.

In her haste to escape the palace, Dunkurian crashed through the windows, shattering the coloured glass as she exited with Zed firmly clamped between her teeth.

Witnessing the vulnerability of her only son, Mrs Brow experienced a flood of flashbacks to when Zed was a little child. The image of him as a defenceless infant resonated with her as she pictured cradling him in her arms as a newborn.

At that moment she knew exactly who that sweet boy was, who was being snatched away. Her mind had cleared the fog caused by being isolated for so long, and she could once again think with clarity. Mrs Brow raced with a superhuman-like velocity. With a powerful skip and an extended hop, she jumped out of the window after them and landed on Dunkurian – straddling her neck.

"Let go of my *baby*!" she demanded. "Release him from your poisonous grasp immediately."

Ignoring Mrs Brow's insistence, Dunkurian flew determinedly over her vast landscape, with Zed screaming and flailing his arms, whilst Mrs Brow continued to urge Dunkurian to cease flying. Mrs Brow repeatedly tugged at Dunkurian's collar, who smirked at Mrs Brow's failed attempts to stop her. Thinking creatively, Mrs Brow reached around to cover Dunkurian's eyes, as a last-ditch attempt to thwart her plan of abduction and bit into the back of the beast's neck as hard as she could.

Dunkurian screamed out in agony, unwittingly releasing Zed from her bite. Feeling disoriented, Dunkurian went hurtling to the ground beneath them. With increasing velocity, they fell downwards. Zed crashed headfirst into the body of water below, swiftly followed by Dunkurian and Mrs Brow, with an immense splash!

Moments later, Mrs Brow resurfaced and searched frantically for her son. She bobbed under the water, only returning to the surface to catch her breath, before submerging herself again… a short while later, Mrs Brow located her precious child and returned his leech-covered body onto the dry land. Hastily removing each of the fluorescent blood-suckers from Zed's face and limbs, she pumped the water out of his lungs to revive him.

Mrs Brow turned him onto his side and then Zed spat out a fat leech, before gasping for air. She had done it. Mrs Brow had successfully revived her son, and she gripped him close, tighter than she had ever held him. At that moment, she appreciated him more than she had in all of his life.

In the distance, Mrs Brow heard what sounded like a motorbike until she realised that the sound was coming from the horizon in the sky. She held her breath and squinted for a moment. At first, she saw a plume of smoke which was swiftly penetrated by the unfamiliar sight of an agricultural plane. Piercing through the clouds was a determined Mr Brow in his crop duster. He often used the plane to fertilize the plants in the palace gardens. Mrs Brow also noticed a youngster beside him with what appeared to be a large, ostrich-sized egg under his arm.

Mrs Brow's attention reverted to the water beside her. It began to bubble and moments later, Dunkurian surfaced from the lake, covered in leeches. Angrier now than she had been earlier, she inhaled deeply in a bid to exterminate Zed and Mrs Brow, but as she breathed out, all that escaped from her mouth was a thin veil of smoke. The Lake of Life had extinguished her flame. At that moment Mr Brow and Hill reached the reservoir.

Zed sprang up from the ground and headed towards his best friend who had landed safely close to the water's edge. He retrieved the highly sought-after egg and stood in front of Dunkurian who was seething.

The Standoff

"Give me my egg!" Dunkurian demanded.

Staring directly into the eyes of a ruthless empress was petrifying. Zed's fear was tapered slightly by having the support of those he cared for nearby. He also trusted Dragio's intimate knowledge of Mirror Maze Land and he believed that Dunkurian would comply with the group's desire to go home, as long as he didn't mess it up. Zed was no stranger to making mistakes, but he only had one chance to get it right. Everyone was relying on him to make it home.

Inhaling deeply, he swallowed hard and muttered his motivational mantra 'You can do this!' before starting. "I know how much this egg means to you." Zed glanced at Dragio, who gave him an encouraging nod to continue. "Probably just about as much as escaping from this place means to me. We have a chance for everyone to win here. If you let us go home, you get to keep this." Zed briefly raised the egg over his shoulder.

The group looked on with bated breath as Dunkurian deliberated.

"I do not make deals with anyone!" she insisted. "Give me one good reason why I shouldn't cast you out to a foreign land for daring to have the audacity to challenge me in my own kingdom?" Dunkurian drew incredibly close to Zed's face. It was something he would never get used to. Her smouldering breath brushed against his cheeks like a gust of desert air. He retreated backwards and his parents stood in front of him, guarding him with their bodies.

"Don't you dare threaten my child!" Mrs Brow warned Dunkurian.

"Haha. Just who do you think you are?"

"First and foremost, I am a parent! You know that fury you are experiencing right now, with my baby holding your egg? Guess what? I feel it too. So immensely. I have not been the best mother to my son and now I have a second chance at doing better; you will not take that opportunity from me. You will not!" she emphasized.

Dunkurian had somewhat admired Mrs Brow's tenacious audacity, and she stepped back to fully assess the situation.

Hill tried to use his charm to stop Dunkurian from feeling alienated and to bring her on-side. "Empress Dunkurian?" He called her by her name to help build a rapport with her. "We recognise you are all-powerful and can do anything you want. All we ask is that you allow us to continue with our lives and friendships back in our own world. Surely you can understand what it's like to miss home?"

"This *is* my home," she retorted.

"I know, and it is a beautiful home. It really is, but it's not our home."

Dunkurian smiled a toothy, insincere grin and reluctantly conceded. "I guess you may have a case. I do have the unique opportunity to get rid of all of you troublesome creatures… So, you want to go home then?"

"Not just us," Zed chipped in. He felt that if he didn't ask at that point, then he never would. Following on from Hill's lead, he probed Dunkurian further. "I bet your magical powers can cross vast lands and landscapes."

Dunkurian chuckled. "Not only do I have the privilege and capability to access realms with my magic, but I can also navigate through timelines. I can delve back into the past."

Of course, Dragio knew that, and he quietly whispered to

Hill, who was the furthest away from Dunkurian's earshot. "The only limitation on her power is that she cannot use magic to transport herself to different realms. This was one of the conditions of her banishment from her homeland."

"We all think it's time for Dragio to go home too, back to the moment just before he discovered Mirror Maze Land." Zed had prompted a wave of support within the group.

"He has served you and this kingdom for a long while now." Hill stuck to his position and continued to reason with Dunkurian.

"I would like that more than anything," Dragio confirmed. "I would love to see my family again. It has been too long."

"Yes, yes, okay, enough of the sob story. Are you all ready?"

Hill and Zed didn't stop to question Dunkurian's apparent change of heart but instead they opted to thank Dragio for helping them along their journey through Mirror Maze Land.

"Say hi to Mama-Bell, from us. We hope to meet her one day!" Hill said.

"Ah." Dunkurian tutted, hinting at a hidden complexity.

"What is it? Mrs Brow probed. Her question was shrouded with suspicion.

"There is an insignificant thing I neglected to add."

"What? What is it?" They all clambered to know.

"If Dragio is to cross both a realm and a timeline, he will have his memory erased and will, therefore, have no recollection of his time here in Mirror Maze Land, which also means that he will forget you… all of you!" Dunkurian delivered the news with an uninhibited smirk.

There was a momentary pause among the group.

Each of them waited for someone else to break the silence.

"I have to do this," Dragio whispered with a sombre expression. He shed a loving tear as he gazed at his companions.

"We know," Zed affirmed.

Hill nodded gently. He couldn't summon the words, but Dragio heard every one of his heartfelt intentions of goodwill.

Mr and Mrs Brow looked on gleefully. Their sweet young boy had been instrumental in giving Dragio his old life back as well as providing them with an opportunity to be better parents to him. They couldn't have been more proud.

Taking in a final breath from Mirror Maze Land air, Dragio felt a flutter of nostalgia. As much as he was desperate to get back to his family, there was a part of him that would miss being a guide in the place that he called home for so long.

"I am ready," he conceded.

With a wave of her reignited tail, Dunkurian decreed, "It is done."

With that, Dragio began to glow a glorious range of fluorescent colours. The tiny little dragonfly then morphed into a young boy. Dragio caught a glimpse of his reflection in the Lake of Life. He had almost forgotten what he looked like in his human form. The admiration only lasted for a fleeting moment, before he glistened even brighter until he transformed into rays of light and disappeared completely.

The remainder of the group stood in formation, ready for Zed to make the final request to leave Mirror Maze Land.

"Wait!" Hill called out. "I would like to make a wish before we depart."

"What? I thought you wanted to go home? Has that changed? You are quite welcome to stay here with me in Mirror Maze Land. I am sure that I can find a use for you… somewhere." Dunkurian smirked.

"Not that, no. I need to explain something to you, Empress Dunkurian. Zed is my very best friend. He has shown great kindness and compassion to me, and he has a tendency to always put others first. At school most people avoid me because of my size. I don't know, I think they are intimidated by me or

115

something. But Zed never once judged me and has, from the very beginning, accepted me for who I am."

Zed's parents looked on tearfully and Hill turned to Zed before continuing, "Zed, I know you've had a hard time looking after yourself." Hill glanced over to Mr and Mrs Brow who appeared sheepish in their expressions. "You've had to worry about when and if you would get a hot meal, which is something that a lot of people our age don't need to think about."

Hill refocussed his gaze on Dunkurian, before making his request. "I would like for my friend not to have to worry about being hungry again."

"I see," Dunkurian confirmed, pausing to consider the request. "Zed, reach into your pocket and pull out the leather wallet."

Zed had developed an understanding of the mysteries of Mirror Maze Land, but he still found that trick incredibly fascinating. He reached into his pyjama pocket and discovered a paper-thin wallet that looked like it was made from snakeskin. He inspected it further and noticed that it glistened and faded to almost invisible, depending on where the light hit. It was mesmerizing.

"Keep this with you and whenever you want currency, from whatever realm you are in, simply place your hand inside and pull the money out. It is a never-ending source. That is a guarantee."

Zed was so pleased and was incredibly grateful to Hill. He would never have thought about asking for financial help, but thanks to the thoughtful nature of his dear friend, he would be the richest eleven-year-old in the world.

Zed's parents could no longer contain their tears, and they sobbed gently.

"Mum, Dad. What's wrong?" Zed handed Dunkurian's egg to Hill and refocused his attention onto his parents.

Mrs Brow mustered the composure to speak. "I am so sorry, Zed, for ignoring you for all those years whilst I was preoccupied with finding treasures. I guess I took you for granted and for that I am truly sorry."

Mr Brow also felt the need to apologise. "We missed you so much, son, and we promise to be better parents. Listening to Hill say all those amazing things about you, makes us happy you finally made a friend, but likewise terribly sad that we let you down."

Lost for words, Zed rushed towards them both with open arms.

"My boy." Mr Brow chuckled, locked in an embrace.

After a short while, Zed turned to Dunkurian, "We are ready to go home."

He signalled to Hill who gently placed Dunkurian's egg on the ground in front of her and said, "Thank you, Empress Dunkurian."

With a farewell nod and a swipe of her tail, Dunkurian decreed, "It is done."

With those ultimate words, Hill, Zed, Mr, and Mrs Brow glistened with the same fluorescent light that Dragio had shone with moments earlier. They gradually faded away until they finally disappeared from Mirror Maze Land.

Stroking her precious egg, Dunkurian gazed knowingly at the spot where the group had departed and smiled.

"Silly humans!"